THE MELON RIND CAFE

THE MELON RIND CAFE

CHINLE MILLER

For Brenda and Aleksandra

———

CONTENTS

Chapter 1	1
Chapter 2	4
Chapter 3	8
Chapter 4	12
Chapter 5	17
Chapter 6	23
Chapter 7	28
Chapter 8	34
Chapter 9	38
Chapter 10	43
Chapter 11	49
Chapter 12	54
Chapter 13	59
Chapter 14	63
Chapter 15	68
Chapter 16	75
Chapter 17	80
Chapter 18	84
Chapter 19	89
Chapter 20	94
Chapter 21	102
Chapter 22	107
Chapter 23	112
Chapter 24	116
Chapter 25	120
Chapter 26	123
Chapter 27	128
Chapter 28	133
Chapter 29	138
Chapter 30	143
Chapter 31	148
Chapter 32	152
Chapter 33	156

Chapter 34   162
Chapter 35   166
Chapter 36   170
Chapter 37   176
Chapter 38   180
Chapter 39   186

About the Author   191

1

Bud Shumway leaned against his old Toyota FJ, watching as a silver and blue Cessna 150 drifted down the nearby runway. He held his breath, hoping the small plane would get up enough acceleration to take off before the runway ended, especially since his wife, Wilma Jean, was in the passenger seat.

The Cessna, which had looked for a moment like it might stall, soon lifted and was airborne like a leaf on a breeze, Bud now breathing a sigh of relief.

It probably would've been fine even if it hadn't taken off, Bud mused, as all it would have to do was make a left-hand turn and cruise the few miles into the little town of Green River, Utah on the old highway, though some of the potholes might give it grief.

Bud was parked by the gate at the Green River Airport, which didn't seem to currently have much going for it, other than a small runway with a few lights, one which was strategically placed where the runway ended, almost at the edge of the old highway. The airport was home to maybe a half-dozen planes, all siblings or cousins of the little Cessna that Bud now watched disappear into the distance.

The small dusty airport didn't even have a fuel pump, and Wilma Jean's first lesson would be conducted while the little plane flew to the nearby town of Radium to gas up. It was a distance of only about 40 air miles, and Bud wondered how much gas it would take just to go get gas.

He'd tried to talk Wilma Jean into going on down to Radium to take flying lessons where they had a real airport, but she wanted to stay in Green River, even though there was no flight school.

Little things like that never stopped his wife, Bud thought, and she'd called her old friend Iris Wells down in Hanksville, asking if her husband Vern would fly up to Green River for a lesson now and then.

Vern was the grandson of one of the early canyon-country aviation pioneers, Gas Wells, who'd been a legend among his fellow pilots, as well as among the many uranium miners he'd flown supplies for. Gas, whose full name was Gaston, was considered by many as the father of canyon-country aviation.

Vern had followed in his granddad's tradition, soloing at the age of 16, and was now himself considered the most knowledgeable back-country pilot in the canyons of southeast Utah. Like his granddad, he flew pretty much everywhere he needed to go, though Iris had a beautiful old green Buick she would sometimes drive to visit the grandkids in Green River.

Bud grinned, the plane now a tiny dot in the distant sky. Vern reminded him of Wilma Jean, the type to always git 'er done, and Bud figured that between the two of them, his wife would have her license in just a couple of days, though he knew that was technically impossible, as the FAA required a set number of hours in the air. He wasn't sure what that number was, but thought Wilma Jean had said 40, so it might actually take them three days.

He opened the FJ door, letting Hoppie and Pierre, the couple's Bassett hound and dachshund, run around in the desert scrub near the airport gate. This was one thing Bud liked about the Green River area—no matter where you went, you were usually the only one there, sometimes even when you were in town.

He again leaned against the FJ, watching the dogs sniff around. He was excited for his wife's newfound passion of flying, as he thought it would be a great way to get into the backcountry. Shoots, they could fly anyplace that had a backcountry strip and go have a picnic, and he could have Wilma Jean fly him over some of the old sites he'd visited as a kid, even to places where he'd worked as a uranium miner.

It then occurred to him that Wilma Jean would have to get a plane, and Bud had no idea what that would cost, though he knew it would probably be a lot more than they could afford. Maybe she could just rent one once in awhile.

Bud now realized he had a knot in his stomach, a feeling of trepidation. Was he worried about Wilma Jean flying? He had to think about it, and yes, there was some concern, but it seemed like he was feeling unsettled more because his world was changing, and not in a minor way.

It felt like something big was about to happen, something big that he might not particularly like, something that could potentially leave him in the dust, just like that little Cessna had left him far behind as it pushed up and away into the wild blue yonder until he was just an insignificant speck far below.

2

Bud absentmindedly kicked at a dead blackbrush with the toe of his Herman Survivors, stirring up dust. The dogs were soon on it, thinking he was after something, digging like mad, kicking up even more dust, their little legs a blur.

He was thinking about how he'd come to be standing by the airport gate waiting for his wife to return, a situation he couldn't have predicted in a million years.

Ever since they'd come back from vacation in Montana where Wilma Jean had learned to fly-fish, she'd been different—kind of restless and talking about how bored she was with running her cafe and bowling alley, the Melon Rind and Tumbleweed Bowl.

It wasn't like her at all, as she was a hard worker and had taken both businesses from basically nothing to success, or such success as one could find in a little windblown town like Green River. In fact, it was her success that had allowed Bud to quit his stressful job as sheriff and become a mellow melon farmer, now managing Krider's Melon Farm.

And even though the melon-farming job ended up paying more than he'd made as sheriff, Wilma Jean had given him the confidence to quit law enforcement when he'd wanted, saying she could support them if necessary.

For her to now make such a 180-degree turn puzzled Bud, as he'd thought she enjoyed her work. But whatever she decided, he wanted to be as supportive of her as she'd been of him, and though he knew he could pay the bills, he was more worried about what she might decide to do next. What if she wanted to become a bush pilot in Alaska or fly cargo to Africa—or go shopping someplace new, like New York City? Who knew where this all might lead?

And now, here he was, waiting as his wife sailed above the big desert in an airplane like some aviatrix flying over the ocean. It made him think of Beryl Markham, the first to fly solo non-stop across the Atlantic from east to west.

The dogs were now, as usual, looking for something to get into, nosing around in a nearby small stand of tamarisk, or tammies as he called them, as if there might be some small critter hiding there.

Bud knew that tammies needed a lot of water, and seeing a stand like this out in the middle of the desert was unusual, as they preferred places like the banks of the Green River.

He'd wondered before how a small stand like this could exist out here by the airport where there was no water and not even a wash that might run occasionally, and he'd once pushed his way into the thicket, where, to his surprise, he'd found a small cold-water geyser.

This had solved the mystery of the plants, but now he wondered why a small geyser would be there. He'd resolved to look into it more, to study the geology. He was familiar with Crystal Geyser, a much bigger cold-water geyser over on the other side of the river a good ten miles distant, and he figured there must be some connection.

For some reason, this country had a number of cold-water geysers, which he knew were rare, unlike the hot-water geysers one finds in seismically active places like Yellowstone. Green River country was about as seismically inactive as a place could get—no threat of earthquakes here, or at least that's what a geologist he'd met up in Montana had told him.

Hoppie and Pierre had now disappeared into the thicket, so Bud pushed his way into the tammies, trying not to get whipped in the face by the long stiff branches. He was soon next to a small mound of red and brown travertine that surrounded a small pool of bubbling water. The dogs were pawing at it playfully, sticking their noses down into what looked like small hot pots, but which Bud knew were actually ice-cold mineral water.

"C'mon, you rascals, it's gonna blow!"

Bud called the dogs, though from the looks of the travertine, the geyser was maybe all of three feet high, maybe less. Just then, Hoppie yelped, holding his paw up.

Bud quickly went to the little dog, hoping he hadn't been bit by a rattler, though he'd seldom seen snakes around, as it was too dry, with little for them to eat.

Patting Hoppie's head, Bud examined his foot, but it didn't look like much more than a scratch. Wondering what had hurt the dog, Bud walked to the edge of the small bubbling pots, where he found a glass jar, a jagged piece broken from its rim, its metal lid gone. The jar had obviously been there awhile, thought Bud, as it was the same color as the travertine around the geyser, making it blend in perfectly.

Hoppie must've stepped on the jar, cutting his foot a little, Bud thought, but what would a canning jar be doing in the geyser? Maybe some old-time cowboy had left it there to keep its contents cool, as canning was about the only way they could preserve food back then.

Bud picked up the jar, slowly dumping out the murky geyser water. He knew that whatever food it once held would be long gone, but to Bud's surprise, something hard rattled in the bottom, and he could now see what looked like a small brown rock. Bud figured it had probably been kicked into the jar by a rabbit or some animal.

Carrying the jar, he made his way back through the tammies to the FJ, the dogs following, where he lifted them back inside. He then dumped the rock into his hand and carefully placed the broken jar on the floor of the FJ so he could take it home and throw it away.

He was ready to toss the rock when he noticed it felt odd—not at all smooth and round, nor was it rough and jagged. It just felt different, though he wasn't sure why.

He held it up to take a closer look, then realized it felt odd because it was faceted, though it was too large to be a jewel. Maybe some rockhound had faceted a piece of quartz, though this particular piece was now reddish brown from the geyser water.

Who knew how long it had been there? Had someone—maybe a geologist—put it in the Mason jar, hoping it would eventually take on the color of travertine, maybe as an experiment?

Bud stuck the rock inside the pocket of his khaki shirt, thinking he would wash it off later and take a closer look, then poured a cup of coffee from his thermos and kicked back in the FJ, waiting for Wilma Jean and Vern to return.

He thought of all the things he needed to do on the farm when he got back, though he knew his most important task for the day would be setting the water and sitting by the ditch, watching the dogs splash around.

He now reached into his shirt pocket and began fiddling with the rock, rolling it in his fingers, wondering again why he felt like something big was about to happen.

It all left him feeling unsettled and wishing he was home, kicked back in his big leather recliner, eating a piece of Wilma Jean's home-made apple pie and reading something comforting, like a model-railroad magazine—or even his camera manual.

3

Something now caught Bud's eye—someone in the distance was walking up the old highway. At first it looked like a mirage, a small stick-like figure in the vast openness of what Bud called the Big Empty, that desert steppe stretching all the way from the Bookcliffs to the San Rafael Reef and on to the distant Henry Mountains in the south.

The Big Empty was misleading in its flatness, as Bud knew it was laced with deep canyons, some of them with impassible slots, and it was sometimes impossible to get from here to there—except in an airplane.

As the figure on the highway got closer, Bud could make out what appeared to be a lone hiker wearing a small backpack.

It was early June, summer in these parts, in spite of the calendar saying it was still spring, and one seldom saw anyone out hiking, as the temperatures could easily top 100 degrees on a typical day.

In fact, there were days when Bud had to go home and wait out the worst of the heat, doing most of his farm work in the early morning and late evening hours, even though the big cottonwoods lining the irrigation ditches on the farm provided some respite.

The figure was now within shouting distance, which it began to do, waving its arms, as if trying to get Bud's attention, even though there was no way Bud could miss seeing him.

"Hey, mister, hey!"

Bud could see it was a guy who looked to be in his early or mid-20s, his wild sandy hair standing straight up as if heavily moussed, though Bud knew it was probably from too many days out camping.

He wore blue jeans with holes in the knees, a dirty t-shirt that read, "It's All Fun and Games Until Someone's Marshmallow Catches Fire," and a brown sneaker on one foot and hiking boot on the other, both with soles that looked like they were delaminating.

"Hey," the young guy said. "Can you tell me how far it is into town? Is there a geyser around here? My name's Duncan."

Bud could now see a vehicle coming up the road in the distance, going much too fast, leaving a rooster tail of dust behind it.

The young man also saw the car, then pointed at the FJ, saying, "It looks like you have an oil leak here. Mind if I crawl underneath and check it out? I'm a pretty good mechanic."

With that, the guy disappeared under Bud's FJ, pack and all, not waiting for Bud to answer.

Soon the vehicle, an old white Ford LTD with faded paint, drove up to the airport gate, around the hanger, then back by the FJ as if looking for something, then slowly drove away. Bud noted it had Utah plates and rode dangerously low to the ground, as if in need of new shocks.

Its driver, a sandy-haired man wearing sunglasses with bright-blue reflective lenses, hadn't looked at or acknowledged Bud, which was considered poor form in canyon country, where strangers always waved to one another. You never knew when you might meet one another more formally later over a flat tire or stuck in deep sand.

A woman with her hair up in blue plastic curlers rode in the passenger seat, and Bud thought he could see someone in the back, though the car's tinted windows prevented him from seeing much. He was only half-paying attention anyway, distracted, wondering why it was taking so long for Vern and Wilma Jean to return, watching for the plane to reappear in the sky.

As the Ford finally disappeared in the distance, Duncan slowly crawled back out from under the FJ.

"Guess I was wrong about the leak," he said congenially. "You work down on that melon farm, don't you? Is that a geyser over in those bushes?"

Bud was startled. How did Duncan know where he worked? He'd never seen him around town or anywhere until now. And how did he know about the geyser?

As if reading Bud's mind, the young guy continued, "I was rafting down the river and saw you working on your farm. Actually, you were sitting by the irrigation ditch playing with your dogs. That's the kind of job I could get into. But is that a geyser?" He pointed towards the tammies.

"It is, but a really small one. Are you a geologist?" Bud asked, but Duncan had already slipped into the tamarisk thicket and was gone. Bud again wondered how he'd known about the geyser, as even most Green Riverites weren't aware of it.

It seemed odd to him, but before he could think much about it, his cell phone rang.

"Yell-ow," Bud answered.

"Hon, it's me," Wilma Jean said. "We're not coming back."

Bud groaned. This was exactly what he'd been afraid of.

She asked, "Hon, you still there?"

"What's going on?" Bud asked with concern, fiddling with the rock.

"We're going up to Price. Can you come get me at the airport there?" she replied. "We're flying a mercy mission. We're taking a golden eagle to the rehab place there. It was hit by a car down by Radium. Since we'll be there anyway, Vern wants to borrow the airport courtesy car and go visit his uncle in the nursing home, assuming you can come get me. He said he doesn't get up there very often and the old guy's not doing too well."

"Sure, I'll get some gas and be there in an hour or so," Bud replied, relieved. "Maybe we can go eat at the Greek Streak. I need to check something on the FJ, then I'll head out."

With that, Bud hung up, grabbed his flashlight from the glove box, then crawled under the FJ, worried about what the young guy had said about a possible leak.

He scanned the bottom of the vehicle, seeing no signs of anything amiss. He was ready to crawl back out when his light reflected off the edge of something small and square stuck up into the frame. He reached up and pulled out what appeared to be a magnetic key holder, slipped it into his pocket, then scooted back out.

Brushing himself off, he distractedly got into the FJ and headed back down the old highway, dodging potholes, dogs now asleep, Hoppie's paw seeming to be OK.

Bud now noticed that the white LTD had stopped by the road a good half-mile ahead as if waiting. That feeling of impending doom washed over him for a moment, but he started humming the old song, "Red River Valley," and it started to go away. He frowned—he was generally an optimist, and feeling unsettled wasn't something he was used to.

As he drove by the LTD, Bud half-expected them to flag him down. Whoever they were, they really didn't belong out in the Big Empty in that car, he mused, as they were sure to get stuck or break an axle. But he knew it was none of his business, especially since they obviously wanted to be left alone. Now looking in his rear-view mirror, he could see that they'd turned around and were headed back towards the airport.

Later, after Bud had stopped in Green River for gas and was back out on the highway on his way to Price, he wondered about Duncan and the geyser and the LTD with its unfriendly passengers, but he decided that he wasn't going to worry about it, for he had places to go and things to do.

His wife had called him to come get her, and he could already taste the best gyros and spanakopita in the whole state of Utah, forgetting all about the rock and key holder in his shirt pocket.

4

"Just what's in this stuff, anyway?" Bud asked Wilma Jean over a plate of dolmades and tzatziki sauce at the Greek Streak. "It's sure good, but I'm not sure I'll like it if I know what I'm eating."

Wilma Jean laughed. "Why wouldn't it taste the same, regardless?"

Bud replied, "Because the human mind is a powerful thing and can override the senses. So if what you're actually eating tastes good but you find it's something you don't like, your brain gets irritated."

"Well," Wilma Jean said, "It's been my experience that about everything that's bad for you tastes good. I don't think most people's brains do a very good job of patrolling things, and it seems like yours can definitely display some serious confusion when it comes to things like vanilla-bean ice cream."

She smiled, then leaned back, suddenly looking thoughtful. Bud frowned, that feeling of impending doom again creeping in from nowhere.

Wilma Jean said, "Hon, I'm really enjoying the flying. It really made me feel good to be able to help Vern get that eagle up here so fast. We saved its life."

"What happened?" Bud asked.

"Well, somebody hit it while it was eating roadkill. They called the wildlife department, who went out and got it and called out to the airport to see if anyone was flying to Price, as that's the nearest wildlife rehab place, Second Chance. It needed to get to a vet ASAP, as it was pretty seriously injured."

She paused to take a sip of tea, then continued. "We'd just gassed up and were ready to take off when the airport manager stopped us. We loaded the eagle, and the rehab people met us here at the airport in Price. They think it's going to survive. Vern says he does stuff like that all the time, but it's usually a mercy flight for people, though he's also transported dogs and cats."

"I thought the Medevac helicopters transported people and had nurses and doctors on board. Is Vern qualified to do that?" asked Bud.

"No, that's emergency stuff. What Vern does is more like taking people from rural areas in for cancer treatments and dialysis, things like that. Sometimes he'll fly relatives up to see someone in a Salt Lake hospital. It's more that kind of thing."

Bud nodded his head. "But who pays for it all? Flying a plane is expensive—gas, maintenance, all that, even if you already own it."

"I'm not sure, but I think there are foundations that help out, and maybe some people's insurance. But hon, I really love flying, and to be able to help people while I'm doing it would just be incredible."

The feeling of doom intensified, and Bud took the rock from his pocket and started fiddling with it beneath the table, where Wilma Jean wouldn't see him. The look in her eyes reminded Bud of a little kid dreaming about getting a pony, and he knew she would soon start talking about buying a plane.

"And you would do all that around here, not someplace like the Yukon?"

Bud absent-mindedly took another bite of dolmades, half afraid of her answer.

"The Yukon? What in the world, Bud Shumway! Are you worried that I'm going to learn to fly and take off for high adventure like Amelia Earhart or something?"

"Well, I sure hope not, at least not the same way she did."

Bud now openly fiddled with the rock, his hands on the table.

"Well, I hope not, too," she said. "By the way, you know what's in your chicken gyro, and your side of dolmades is just grape leaves stuffed with hamburger and rice, and tzatziki is a cucumber dip, just so you know. My spanakopita is just spinach on a pita. And the Greek Streak doesn't serve ice cream. You'll have to have a piece of baklava if you want dessert."

"Or wait till we're home and have warm apple pie with vanilla-bean ice cream on top," Bud grinned, relieved that his wife wasn't thinking of flying to some distant horizon.

He then continued, trying to distract her and end the conversation before it got a tad expensive. "I need to get back to the farm and change the water—that field's probably good and soaked by now. We'll want to stop and walk the dogs for a few minutes, too, so we should be going."

"Are you fiddling again?" Wilma Jean laughed. "What is it this time?"

"What do you think this is?" Bud wiped the rock on a napkin, some of the travertine coming off, then handed it to Wilma Jean.

"It looks like a rock, hon," she replied. "A brownish red rock. Is it something important?"

"No, I think it's a piece of quartz, but notice how it appears to have been faceted? I think that's kind of odd."

She held it up to the light, then handed it back to him, saying, "It's probably something a rockhound did, and Lord only knows that could be anyone in Green River. Where did you find it?"

"Out at the geyser by the airport."

"I didn't know there was a geyser out there. Where is it?"

"It's where all those tammies are growing, just across from the gate."

"No kidding?"

Bud thought again of Duncan and the people in the Ford LTD. Maybe he'd drive back out there after he set the water and see if they'd gotten stuck. He then remembered the key holder in his pocket and thought about opening it, then decided it might be better not to do it in the restaurant, for who knows what it might hold.

Wilma Jean, not to be sidetracked, added, "Hon, before we go, there's one more thing..."

Bud now started humming an old song by the Sons of the Pioneers, "Tumbling Tumbleweeds," trying to distract himself from that feeling of doom, which had started to go away, but was now back, hanging on for dear life.

He said with urgency, "We really need to go, hon. Can't we discuss it later?"

"We can, but carpe diem, or maybe I should say carpe moment. You'll get busy and I won't see you until late because I have to be at the cafe all evening. Bud, I want to buy my own plane, and you know that's not going to be cheap."

Bud sighed. Well, there it was, and it wasn't the end of the world. Why had he felt so doomed? He needed to get a grip on himself and stop being so dramatic. But the feeling hadn't abated and was in fact getting even stronger.

Wilma Jean continued, "And if I'm out flying, I won't have time to run things, and Maureen and Howie are thinking about taking over Howie's Drive-In, as the buyer defaulted on it, so she won't be working for me anymore."

Bud absentmindedly slipped from the booth and stood, knowing that the world he'd come to love was about to end—no more stopping by the cafe for meatloaf and mashed potatoes anytime he got hungry, or at least not for free.

Wilma Jean said, "I want to put the Melon Rind and bowling alley up for sale, and I realize this will be a huge change for us both, but I really think I can get my pilot's license pretty fast. Vern says I'm a natural. Hon, think about it and let me know how you feel. I want to put it on the market right away."

Bud was now aware of how impatient he must appear standing there while his wife discussed what could be the most important change in her life, so he sat down in the booth next to her as if that was what he'd planned to do all along, putting his arm around her.

He tried to act casual, even though the feeling of doom now had him by the neck. He would sure miss her homemade apple pie.

"You know," he said, squeezing her shoulder, "You've always been there for me, no matter what, through my ups and downs. I don't need to think about this. If that's what you want to do, you have my full support, 100 percent. I've always thought you would find something else, that running the cafe and bowling alley didn't match your talents, and if you want to fly, I think it's great. We can get a loan for the plane so you can start flying before you sell everything."

Wilma Jean, now excited, added, "We can sell the Airstream for part of the money if we need to. My cousin Juno would loan me the rest—I know he would."

"Juno buying a plane would be like me buying a new camera lens," Bud replied. "Hardly a dent in the pocketbook. We'll make it work, but let's get on back."

With that, he again stood, left enough cash on the table to pay for their bill and tip, and quickly walked out the door, wanting desperately to go see Hoppie and Pierre, who patiently waited in the FJ.

He knew the wag of their tails and grins on their little faces would tell him all would be OK, as he slipped them each a piece of chicken smuggled from his gyro. And maybe he could talk Wilma Jean into making up a bunch of pies and freezing them before she sold the cafe.

Somehow, it would all work out, he figured, the sense of doom now gradually fading as he patted their little heads.

5

Bud sat with his back against a big cottonwood, watching as Hoppie and Pierre took a dip in the irrigation ditch. Hoppie was tall enough to stand on the bottom, but the little dachshund was too short and had to swim or he would float on down. Every once in awhile Pierre would come out to rest, but he'd soon be back in, barking madly when he'd see Hoppie chasing a leaf or stick floating down the water.

Bud smiled at their antics, even though he was distracted, trying to figure out how a tumbleweed could be a landmark on a map. By definition, tumbleweeds moved, so trying to anchor something using a tumbleweed seemed futile. He'd at first thought the name might refer to his wife's business, Tumbleweed Bowl, but that didn't make sense either.

He again took the key holder from his pocket and opened it, taking out a small piece of folded paper. It sure looked like a map of some kind, he thought, though it was pretty cryptic, just a bunch of scrawled lines connecting barely decipherable letters—C, TM, PTM, T, TS, BB, LB, SS, C/C, A—except for the word, "Tumbleweed," which was where the lines originated and radiated from like arrows.

If it were some kind of map, he thought, why not show a road or two, or give someone something more substantial to go by than a tumbleweed?

He turned the paper upside down, wondering if it could be some kind of scientific sketch, like maybe a chart of the electrons around a tumbleweed atom. The problem with that theory, Bud mused, was that it would be a very lopsided atom, for most of the lines were on one side of the tumbleweed, and besides, even a grade-school graduate knew that tumbleweeds had more than one atom.

There was one other thing, though, and that was a couple of lines written in an almost illegible scrawl at the bottom:

Follow the lines, give each a day, and a stubborn Scot can fly away.

Bud folded the paper back up and put it in his pocket where the rock still resided, then began fiddling with the key holder for a moment. He thought for awhile, then crawled under the FJ, putting the holder back where it had been up in the frame. The dogs jumped from the ditch, thinking it was time to go home, shaking water all over Bud as he crawled back out.

He was sure beyond a doubt that Duncan had put the key holder under his FJ, though he had no idea why. But for some reason, Bud suspected that Duncan might just come back for it, as he apparently knew where Bud worked. And when he did, maybe he would explain to Bud what was going on, since Bud now had the map in his pocket.

He sat back down under the tree, the dogs happily returning to the water. He needed to think, and there was no hurry to get home, as Wilma Jean was at the cafe.

If the paper were a map of some kind, why put it in a key holder under a stranger's vehicle? Had Duncan been carrying it under his own vehicle and broken down out in the desert? Breaking down this time of year could be a disaster, but why would he have a map in a key holder in the first place? Was he trying to hide it because someone was after it?

He thought again of the people in the Ford LTD. They had seemed suspicious—were they looking for Duncan? Was that why he'd slipped under the FJ, to hide the key holder and also himself?

What could he possibly have that they wanted, unless it was the map? And why would anyone care about a tumbleweed?

It was all too confusing, and Bud had a sudden urge to go home and take a nap in his big leather recliner.

Just then, a forest-green Land Cruiser drove up, the words, "Emery County Sheriff," lettered on the door, lights on and siren blaring. A tall lanky man in desert-sand khakis with emblems on his shoulders stepped out, saying, "You're under arrest, Sheriff."

Bud nodded, grinning. It was Howie, who still referred to Bud as sheriff, even though it had been some time since he'd resigned that post in Howie's favor.

"What did I do, Sheriff?" Bud asked.

"Dogs fishing without a license, Utah State Statute 107-02, and weener dogs get fined double, since the fish think they're one of them and swim right up, making them easier to catch."

Bud laughed. "What's the fine?"

Howie answered, "You have to share the fish. But hey, Bud, you have to read this. I've noticed more people in town lately, and this explains why. I mean, I saw five people get off the train yesterday, when there's usually only one or two."

Howie sat down under the tree by Bud, handing him what looked to be the latest issue of *Treasure Magazine*. The cover had a photo of a big metal box with what appeared to be Spanish coins spilling out and an elderly square-jawed gent looking down on it with obvious satisfaction. A headline in bold letters read, "Mackie's Treasure Finally Revealed!"

It all looked vaguely Photoshopped to Bud.

"Open it up!" Howie demanded.

Inside, Bud read:

Mackie Finally Admits to Burying Million-Dollar Treasure, Gives Major Clues to Location

Angus Mackie, who made a fortune in automatic tire-pressure detectors after prospecting in the desert and having numerous flats, today revealed for the first time that he had indeed buried part of his fortune, as has long been suspected by those familiar with his distaste for banks.

Mackie is rumored to be worth many millions, and he told Treasure Magazine that he had converted most of his fortune to rare gold coins found by Cortez himself and taken to Spain. When Mexico demanded repatriation, the coins were sent to the United States for safe-keeping, where they were supposedly stolen by Butch Cassidy, eventually making their way into the hands of a private coin collector.

Interesting how they got Butch Cassidy in there, Bud grinned. Good old Butch—always good for about anything that needed stealing, and pretty convenient for him that the coins had been sent to the U.S. for safekeeping. He continued reading.

Not trusting banks, Mackie buried the treasure some years ago in country where he once prospected for uranium. He recently decided that, instead of telling only his family where it was hidden, he would make it a game open to anyone, and whoever was clever enough to find it could have it.

"It's the spirit of the chase," said the elderly Scotsman, who's well-known for both his bagpipe playing and his droll sense of humor. "My family has everything they need, so I want to open this up to everyone. If someone in my family finds it first, well, so be it, but I want to assure everyone that they know no more about it than anyone else."

"It's in a strongbox, so is well-protected from the elements, and I can tell you that you'll see the most valuable thing ever when you open that box, assuming you're the one to find it. The poem I'm giving you has every discovery clue you need, and in the spirit of returning it to Butch's home country of Utah, I've hidden it near Green River. Good luck, everyone."

For a mere $50, Treasure Magazine will send you a laminated copy of Mackie's poem, guaranteed to withstand whatever may come your way while out treasure hunting. A portion of these funds will be put in a special account to help the survivors of those lost while looking."

Bud closed the magazine, whistling. "Woo-eee! How many do you think are gullible enough to send their hard-earned cash for a poem?"

He immediately regretted saying anything, seeing the look on Howie's face, who had just pulled a small laminated piece of paper from his pocket.

"Well, the way I look at it, Sheriff," Howie said measuredly, "Is that most of that money is probably going to the families of the remaining. If I can even half-figure this poem out—and I've got Old Man Green and Junkyard Goldie working on it—it's not going to be in an easy place to get to. And I'm worried a lot about who's going to have to pick up the pieces of missing treasure hunters. I know it's going to be me, unless I can find it first and call off the chase."

Bud grinned. "So, let me see if I understand this correctly, Sheriff. It would be in the line of duty—shoots, maybe even above and beyond the line of duty because of how risky it could be—if you were to find this lost treasure yourself, is that correct?"

"That's correct, Sheriff," Howie grinned. "I knew my metal detector would come in handy some day, and when I do find it, we're all going to retire young, you and me and Maureen and Wilma Jean."

"That's really nice of you, Howie, but it's too late," Bud replied grimly.

Howie looked concerned. "Why is that?"

"Because none of us are what you would call young any more," Bud smiled. "Way too late."

Howie replied, "Better late than never. But I just hope that treasure isn't out in Little Area 51."

"You mean the old missile base? Since when is it called Little Area 51?"

"That's what's on the Google maps now, Bud. But I've had several calls recently of people seeing spacemen out there. I'm trying to stay away from that place, at least at night, as that's when the calls come in, though I did go out there yesterday for a few minutes."

"Spacemen? Like in little green ET-type spacemen?"

"No, Bud, real spacemen, the kind in big white spacesuits with helmets that ride in rockets. You're thinking of aliens, but these are spacemen. If you watched enough sci-fi movies, you'd know the difference. Spacemen want to steal Earth's minerals and stuff like that, whereas aliens just want a snack—preferably a human snack."

"Maybe they're looking for Mackie's treasure. Did you see any tracks or anything odd out there?"

Howie replied, "No, but the farthest I went was out to the tent slabs, and that was in broad daylight. There's lots more to the base than that, it's huge. But everyone said they saw them near the slabs. But there weren't any tracks, unless you count antelope tracks, nothing unusual. Call me inept and not doing my job, but only if you go with me will I go out there at night."

"Well, maybe I can go out there with you this evening," Bud offered, jumping up as the dogs came over and started shaking water everywhere. "But for now I should probably go tell Wilma Jean to expect a big upturn in business from hungry treasure hunters. Let's go have dinner at the Melon Rind—we'll go fill up on good food and say goodbye to our wives before the spacemen abduct us—or would that be more like aliens?"

6

Bud and Howie leaned against Bud's FJ, watching the last sunrays disappear behind the jagged-tooth silhouette of the San Rafael Reef to the west. Bud was wishing he'd brought his camera, as it had been a spectacular sunset, with reds and golds and maroons lining huge cumulus clouds that appeared to be coming their way.

"It's a bit early for the monsoons," Bud mused.

"It does look like a big wet one coming in, doesn't it?" Howie replied. "Might slow down the treasure hunters."

"Yes, and I could've maybe got a good sunstar photo right as it went over the rim, right under that cloud bank, if I'd only brought my camera. Would've been a great shot."

"A sunstar? Did you see one?" Howie asked. "I've actually never seen a sunstar."

Bud laughed. "That's because you can only see them through the camera lens, Howie. You have to set your aperture real small to capture them."

"I always wondered about that, Bud," Howie said. "I mean, I've seen some spectacular pictures of sunstars, but never could actually manage to see one. I always thought I wasn't in the right place at the right time. Now I know why."

The moment the sun set, the night chill began to move in, and Bud and Howie got back into the FJ, kicking back, feeling a little stuffed from dinner at the Melon Rind.

One of the nice things about Green River country, Bud thought—shoots, maybe most of the West—was that the night almost always cooled off quickly, no matter how hot the day had been. He knew it was from the lack of humidity, and even the monsoon clouds didn't affect it much.

Bud had taken the dogs home earlier, given them their dinner and turned on some lights, as he knew he'd be getting in after dark. Now there was nothing to do but wait and see if any spacemen decided to pay them a visit.

Just to their east sat a number of small concrete slabs, built for tent bases by the military during the heydays of the Green River Launch Complex in the 1960s and 70s. The complex, a big economic boon to Green River at the time, had sent many sleek white Athena missiles to the waiting arms of the White Sands Missile Base in New Mexico.

A few of the guys who had worked there were still around and were getting pretty elderly, though most moved away when the base closed in 1979. Bud had seen a couple of them just that afternoon, old Joe Anderson and Winn Day, over in the city park by the commemorative Athena missile there, probably talking about the good old days.

Now, as it got dark, Bud noticed that Howie had locked his door. Sure enough, he said, "Bud, I think you should lock your door."

Bud locked it, wondering what good it would do since they had their windows down to let in the cool air.

Howie sighed. "I have some bad news, Bud. You know how we talked about getting into model railroading when you guys came back from your Montana vacation? You know I'm still interested, but I want to get a better amp for my guitar. When I find the treasure I can afford to do both, but right now I need the amp worse. The band must play on."

"I've been kind of thinking the same thing, Howie. I'd like to get a new lens for my camera, and the one I want won't be cheap," Bud replied.

Howie sighed. "We're on the same track, Sheriff. Gee, I never thought about it much, but you know, we have one big thing in common."

"What's that, Howie?"

"We're both artists—you're a photographer and I'm a musician. And if we buy all this stuff we want, we'll be starving artists."

Bud replied, "Well, you know what they say about that, don't you?"

"Not really."

Bud grinned. "They say an artist is someone who can starve to death without actually dying."

Howie studied the fading hills beyond the slabs as if looking for spacemen. "I never thought about it that way, Bud, but I do know we'll never starve as long as there's the Melon Rind, well, and Howie's, too, since we're going to reopen it."

Bud paused for a moment, then said, "Howie, I don't know if Wilma Jean's told you guys, but she wants to sell the cafe."

Howie turned and looked at Bud, now silhouetted against the starry sky. "No kidding? Jeez Louise. No, I didn't know that. That's pretty big news. I'm surprised it's not all over town."

Bud replied, "She just decided. With you guys taking back Howie's Drive In, she won't have Maureen to help run it, and she's been wanting to get free from it all anyway. Krider's daughters used to help some, but they're both off to college now. She's burned out, kind of like I was when I quit the sheriff's job. She wants to become a pilot."

"A pilot? Isn't that kind of dangerous?" Howie asked.

Bud replied, "Yeah, and it does worry me, Howie."

"Too much change going on around here, Sheriff," Howie said.

Bud leaned out the window, looking up at the stars. The Milky Way shimmered above like a tiara of diamond dust.

""I forgot you're an astronomy buff, Howie," Bud said. "You should've brought your telescope. No wonder you know the difference between aliens and spacemen. But where exactly is Sagittarius, anyway?"

Howie pointed through the windshield. "See that teapot shape up there? That's it. Why?"

Bud replied, "I'm starting to get into night-sky photography, and Sagittarius is towards the galactic center of the Milky Way, where the stars are thickest, the best direction to get photos."

Howie said, "It's almost the solstice, then Sagittarius will be at its highest in July, which would be the best time to shoot the Milky Way. A lot of people don't realize that part of the galaxy dips below the horizon in the fall and winter."

They were silent for awhile, then Howie asked, "You're going to keep working for Krider, aren't you?"

Bud answered, "I'll still be melon farming. No reason to quit. I'll have to pay all the bills until Wilma Jean gets some experience, though selling the cafe and bowling alley will give us a buffer—well, maybe not, since she wants to buy a plane. But I wouldn't know what to do with myself if I wasn't doing something or other, Howie."

"You could become a professional photographer," Howie suggested.

Bud laughed. "Well, that sure doesn't seem very likely, especially around Green River. Only so many photos one can sell of cliffs and desert."

"Bud, you could come work for me. I keep telling the mayor I need a deputy. When I'm out and about, there's nobody to cover for me. It can get tough, you know. You didn't have this problem when you were sheriff, 'cause you had me as your deputy."

"Well, that's true, but there sure isn't much going on most of the time, and I'm always around if you need me. You can also call the State Patrol when you need backup for something serious."

Howie answered, "Except they're usually way out somewhere else and can't get here in time. And it's more psychological, Bud, you know that. I take my job pretty darn seriously, and it bothers me when I'm out chasing Old Man Green's cows off the road to know something really big could be coming down the pike and there's nobody to cover for me. I don't want my constituents to think I'm a bad sheriff."

"I'm sure they don't, Howie," Bud replied. "They elected you, didn't they? But say, this would be a good time to take a look at that treasure poem you bought. I'd be curious to see if I can make any connections."

"I stopped by the house to check on the cats on my way to the cafe and left it there, Bud. Don't want anything to happen to it. We can go over it together later."

Now they both sat, silently looking out their windows at the immensity of the sky over the Big Empty with its endless stars, each lost in their own thoughts, Bud fiddling with the rock in his pocket.

Finally, Howie said softly, "Maureen says we're gonna make it big someday with the band..."

His voice trailed off as he noticed something white coming up from the shadows at the slabs, something with big puffy arms and legs and a big bulbous head.

Speechless, Howie tried to warn Bud by tugging on his arm, but it was too late. The spaceman now stood at Bud's window in his big white spacesuit, looking at them through what appeared to be a plex-iglass helmet that reflected the stars.

It slowly moved its puffy arm, pointing at the dirt road back to town, and spoke in a scratchy metallic voice that sounded like it came from depths far away.

"Would you mind leaving so we can do our work?"

Bud managed to mumble, "You bet," then quickly turned the FJ key and drove away.

7

"We may have the distinction of being the first on Earth to communicate with a spaceman," Bud said, easing down into a big overstuffed chair at Howie and Maureen's. "He sure spoke good English, didn't he? I hope we don't give him any of our Earth viruses—or vice versa."

Howie, a bit shaky and obviously still recovering from the incident, handed Bud a cup of hot chocolate.

"You're sitting in Bodie's chair, Bud, so don't be surprised if he tries to sit in your lap. You sound like you don't believe that spaceman was real."

"Oh, he was real enough," Bud replied, holding the cup in one hand and petting the big Maine coon cat, who was now in his lap, with the other. "But the odds of him speaking such good English seem pretty slim, don't you agree?"

"If they're smart enough to get to Earth, why not be smart enough to learn the language?" Howie asked. "They probably can pick up transmissions and study English that way, sort of like the Russians do. But you know, I think they may be in the wrong Green River. They want Green River, Wyoming."

"Why is that?"

"Because that's where the spaceport is."

"Spaceport?"

"The Greater Green River Intergalactic Spaceport," Howie replied.

"Seriously?"

"Yeah, it's a dirt strip a few miles from Green River up on the mesa there." Howie sat down on the couch across from Bud, his other Maine coon cat, Tobie, jumping into his lap.

"Do they get much intergalactic traffic?" Bud asked, sipping his hot chocolate, Bodie now trying to knead his leg.

"It's kind of a joke, but maybe not so much, once word gets out to the rest of the galaxy," Howie replied. "See, Green River heard about the potential collision of Comet Shoemaker-Levy 9 with Jupiter—this was back in the mid-1990's when NASA was tracking it. The town decided, in the spirit of intergalactic friendship, to create a landing strip for the poor and homeless refugees from Jupiter, or Jovians, as they're called. They put up a sign and a windsock, but so far, no spacemen have shown up, at least not that they know of. It's actually an FAA-approved airstrip with its own designation code and everything. Last I heard, private pilots land there every once in awhile just to say they did."

"I'll have to tell Wilma Jean about it," Bud laughed. "But Howie, something tells me that our particular spaceman is from Earth. I think the Air Force or NASA or someone is out there messing around and they don't want anyone to know about it."

"Well, they're not keeping a very low profile, since we're about the fourth ones now to see them. I wonder what they would've said if we'd been in the patrol vehicle. Seems like they wouldn't be telling the sheriff to just scoot."

"Well, you're assuming they can read, but you'll have to go back out there and see," Bud answered. "But it's getting late. Let's take a quick look at that poem."

"It's not really something you can look at real quick, Bud. It's pretty complicated. But hang on."

Howie dumped Tobie from his lap and disappeared for a

moment, then returned with a sheet of laminated paper, saying, "Let me read it out loud to you. It flows a little better that way."

"And you say you have some of it interpreted?" Bud asked.

"Some of it. But let's look at the first stanza."

> *You want the riches, treasure trove,*
> *Whose gold will bring you many things,*
> *But stop and ponder on it now,*
> *Before you risk its deadly stings.*

"See, it's telling us to be careful, as you might get what you wish for, and it might not be what you want after all. I've heard that about lottery winners, that it changes their lives, and not necessarily for the better. And I think I have the interpretation for the deadly stings— that would be things like scorpions and rattlers. Now, let's look at the next one."

> *Begin the search away from rim,*
> *Where light shines up the canyon wall,*
> *From Tumbleweed go 'round the bend,*
> *And you will see where you can't fall.*

"He's telling us it's not on a canyon rim, but away from it. But, well, that's all the further I got, Bud, I've only had it a few days."

"Tumbleweed?" Bud mused, thinking again of the cryptic map in his pocket. He touched the rock, making sure it was still there.

Howie replied, "I think he's saying it's not someplace where you'll find tumbleweeds—the problem with that, though, is that it eliminates most of this country, heck, most of Utah or even the West. And I don't get the part about light shining up the canyon wall."

"Howie, I think that might refer to water. Haven't you ever seen the river reflect light onto the canyon walls above?"

"Hot dog, Sheriff, I think you may be right, and that's not so close to the rim, it's actually down below it. And you can't exactly fall when you're on the water, can you? And it would explain the start of the next stanza, *It's not a place where one walks free,* 'cause you can't walk on water, though I know a few people who think they can. No wonder you're such a good detective, Bud. Maybe you can help me solve this thing."

"It might be fun to try," Bud replied.

"Here's the next one," Howie continued.

> *It's not a place where one walks free,*
> *But if you search at setting sun,*
> *You'll see the man high in the scree,*
> *His left arm points where search is done.*

"That one really puzzles me, Bud. What could a man high in the scree mean? Does he have someone out there who will show you where it's at if you get close? It doesn't make sense. Anyway, here's the rest."

> *You cannot walk, you cannot swim,*
> *You must have wood beneath your feet,*
> *And treasure bright will be too dim,*
> *To guide your light for shore to meet.*

> *If you are wise and find the way,*
> *Across the hazards as they flow,*
> *Beware of slippery feet of clay,*
> *Walk soft and take in sunset glow.*

> *So do it now, and if you fail,*
> *You know your life will be at stake,*
> *For June it is, you've heard the tale,*
> *And summer solstice is the take.*

> *The brave will win, the fool will die,*
> *And which you are you soon will know,*
> *For nothing here can be a lie,*

And fool's gold treasure lies below.

"Wow," Bud said. "That makes my head spin."

Just then, his phone rang.

"Yell-ow," he answered, then paused, listening, and said, "Howie's right here. I'll give him the message. Is the Radium SAR crew on their way? OK, give me the coordinates."

Bud listened some more, taking a pen and paper from his pocket and writing numbers down, then said, "We'll be right there, Hum. I'll call you if we need help," and hung up.

"Howie, that was Sheriff Hum down in Radium. Some rafters dialed 911 and the signal bounced down his way. I'm surprised it got out of the canyon at all. They're camped on the river and can hear someone calling over and over for help, and it's coming from the cliffs above. They think there may be more than one person stuck, as they were yelling, 'Help us!' Hum gave me the coordinates, as they have a GPS. Let's look it up and get out there and see what we can see. Radium SAR is on standby in case we need them, but they're a good hour or more away."

Howie pulled out his GPS and entered the coordinates Bud had written down.

"It's Lover's Leap, Bud. I've always wondered when I'd get a call from out there. The rafters must be camped on that sand bar right under it. If this person is up in the cliffs, we'll need search and rescue for sure. Radium has a good high-angle team."

Bud knew Howie was referring to a place not far from the airport where a small road ended a good 600 feet or so right above the river. For some reason, Howie always called it Lover's Leap, though Bud had never heard anyone else call it that. He'd been there a few times trying to get photos of the river far below, but they'd never turned out, as there was too much contrast between the river and the canyon shadows.

"Let's go!" Howie said, excited. "I'll take the Land Cruiser and you can follow me in your FJ, and that way if one of us has problems we're not stuck out there."

"Problems?" Bud asked. "Howie, it's a good road, and only a few miles from town. We're not likely to have any problems, unless..."

"Spacemen problems, Bud," Howie said, locking the house door behind them. "Lover's Leap is close to the old missile base. They may want to steal my GPS or something—who knows what their devious minds might come up with?"

8

Bud had rolled up the FJ windows, not wanting to eat Howie's dust as
he followed him down the dusty River Road that led from town into
the desert. He could barely make out the *Road Impassible When Wet*
sign where they split off from the Airport Road, and he decided to let
Howie get a ways ahead so the dust would settle some.

It was then that he saw headlights coming from the opposite
direction, and he slowed, giving them plenty of space. It was rare to
see anyone out here, and he wondered if it weren't some treasure
hunter getting back late.

They were soon upon him, going much too fast for the conditions,
and he could see through the swirling dust for but a brief moment,
but what he saw gave him pause—it was the old white Ford LTD.

What in the world were they doing way out here at this time of
night? Did they know something about the person calling for help in
the cliffs?

Bud stepped on it and caught up to Howie just as the Land
Cruiser turned off on the road to Lover's Leap. The road gradually
climbed for a couple of miles, then dead-ended a few yards from the
cliff's edge at some large rocks.

Bud and Howie both got out, the swirling dust settling around them, and walked to the edge of the cliff.

"Careful," Bud said. "It goes straight off."

"Listen," Howie replied, shining his big sheriff's flashlight all around. "I think I hear something."

"Be careful, Howie," Bud repeated.

He knew that, in spite of Howie's fears of spacemen and such, he could be fearless when it came to his own safety. He recalled once when Howie had climbed down the cliffs above the San Rafael River to rescue a woman who'd fallen partway into the treacherous Black Box. He'd saved her life in what had been a harrowing and ropeless rescue.

Bud wasn't particularly interested in repeating the experience, especially since part of the rescue had involved the woman grabbing onto his feet for dear life as Howie hoisted her up, almost pulling Bud into the abyss.

Now Bud could hear the faint sound of someone calling out, someone who sounded weak and disoriented.

"Help!"

Bud carefully made his way to the edge, holding on to a large boulder, shining his light into the depths. He then shone his light along the rim. "Howie, I think they're up here."

"There's something white over there," Howie said. "Bud, if it's another one of those spacemen..."

"Howie, I think it's someone with white hair."

Bud and Howie were soon next to where a man lay on the ground, face down, only a few feet from the cliff edge, groaning. Bud carefully turned him over, noting he had blood on his forehead, but afraid to move him more in case he had a spinal injury.

Bud spoke in a whisper so the old guy couldn't hear him.

"Howie, he appears to be in shock. He's bleeding pretty badly from that head wound. We need to get on this fast. Call the Medevac chopper, then get the first-aid kit."

Howie was soon on the phone while Bud talked to the older guy, asking him if he was OK and trying to reassure him, even though he was pretty much unresponsive.

Howie, now opening the first-aid kit, whispered, "Bud, this looks like the same guy as on the cover of *Treasure Magazine*, Angus Mackie."

"It certainly does, Howie," Bud replied grimly.

The old guy started moaning, motioning for them to come close.

"Hang in there, Mr. Mackie," Howie said, gently putting his hand on the old man's arm. "We're getting you to a hospital right away."

"I don't need a hospital," wheezed the old man. "Damn witch's tongue. But would you get a message to my grandson? Tell him that Tumbleweed's a..."

And with that, he groaned, closed his eyes, and passed into another realm.

Bud sighed, wondering where old Scotsmen go when they die. He began CPR while Howie felt for a pulse, but after awhile, he knew it was too late.

Bud said, "Might as well cancel that chopper and instead get the ambulance from Green River for a body recovery."

Howie placed his jacket over the old man.

They both stood there in silence, then finally turned and walked back to their vehicles, where Howie cancelled the Medevac chopper and instead called the ambulance.

Bud and Howie then sat on a big nearby rock, looking up at the stars, silently waiting for the Green River EMS team to arrive.

Bud couldn't help but wonder if what had happened to the old Scotsman had anything to do with gold fever, and if maybe Howie hadn't been right to worry about picking up the pieces from an inundation of treasure hunters.

The ambulance finally arrived, taking the old man away, but Bud and Howie lingered, not sure how to break the feeling of doom and finality that surrounded the Scotsman's death.

Neither felt like going home, instead needing to process what had just happened. They sat for some time, pondering the meaning of life and all its ups and downs, gazing into the night sky.

Finally, after watching a blue-white meteor streak across the horizon, Bud said, "Howie, I didn't want to worry you, but Hum said the rafters told him they'd seen something really odd. He wasn't sure whether or not to even call us, as he wondered if they weren't drinking, but he decided to err on the side of caution."

Howie asked, "What did they see?"

Bud replied, "Two beings in white spacesuits, right down on the beach by Crystal Geyser."

"Oh man," Howie groaned.

"But there's more," Bud added. "It looked like they were roasting hotdogs over a fire. The spacemen waved at them as they floated past. The rafters swore they hadn't been drinking."

Howie replied, "I think we'd better get on home, Bud." He stood, adding, "But how they could eat hotdogs through those big helmets is a mystery to me."

9

Bud watched as the little Cessna 150 again took to the skies, holding his breath until it cleared the old highway, though not quite as nervous as at Wilma Jean's first lesson. Vern had said it would be a short flight, as the clouds building up to the west were of some concern.

Bud waited until the plane was far over the canyons to the east, then got into his FJ and headed for what Howie called Lover's Leap.

He wanted to go back and look for clues as to what might have happened to Angus Mackie the previous night, hopefully before something destroyed them. Howie couldn't go until later, as he was fixing the headlight on his patrol vehicle, having had what he'd called an "incident" on his way back to town.

Bud had left the dogs at home, as it was getting too hot for them to wait in the FJ, plus he didn't want them around the big cliffs. He had a little experiment he wanted to conduct from the edge.

He parked at the end of the road next to the big rocks and got out, binoculars over his shoulder and camera in hand. He first walked around the parking area, looking at the vehicle tracks, though he knew that between him and Howie and the ambulance, any clues were probably long gone.

He knew what his FJ tracks looked like, as well as those of the patrol vehicle, and the ambulance track was also pretty easy to identify from the wider tires. But he wanted to know if anyone else had driven up there, and just as he suspected, he found another set of tracks that he thought might match an older Ford LTD.

Examining the LTD tracks more closely, there were places where they were underneath the others, which meant that the LTD had been there before he and Howie showed up. This would match perfectly time-wise with Bud seeing the people in the LTD on their way back to town.

Now he recalled when he'd seen the car out by the airport with a third figure in the back. Had that person been Angus Mackie? Had they driven out to the rim here to kill the old man, then returned to town?

Whatever had happened, Bud knew that at this point any evidence he found was purely circumstantial. He next walked around the big rocks, looking for more tracks and being careful not to obliterate what was there.

He knew the tall cliffs were Cedar Mountain Formation, mudstones and silts laid down by an ancient lake and bearing the bones of dinosaurs. In his experience, it was always easy to track people through this kind of dirt, as it was more like a loose unconsolidated dried mud than sand.

He walked around, gradually working his way to where they'd found Angus, and it was near there that he found what appeared to be a melee of tracks made from several different types of footwear, one of which appeared to be a woman's, smaller and with pointed toes.

A separate set of tracks seemed to meander to where Angus had been, as if he'd wandered away from the others. Now Bud saw tracks closer to the rim, almost wearing a small path going back and forth. They appeared to be the same as those he'd found over by where the car had been parked—a man and a woman's.

He took a few pictures, but found nothing more of interest, so went and sat on a large rock on the rim. It was time for his experiment, and he held his binoculars to his eyes, scanning the river below. He knew that June was a prime time for rafters and canoeists on the Green, so it was just a matter of time before someone showed up.

Sure enough, it wasn't long until he saw two canoes coming down the river. Still watching through the binoculars, he yelled out, "Hello down there!"

The canoeists made no motion as if they'd heard him, so he yelled even louder, "Hellooooo!"

There was still no look of recognition, so Bud finally yelled in his loudest voice, "Anybody awake down there?"

Now he could see that both canoeists were looking in his direction, so he stood and waved his arms. Sure enough, they began waving back.

"Helloooo," he yelled again, and now they yelled, "Helloooo." It was faint, but he could make out what they were saying.

Bud sat back down on the rock, wondering how someone on the river could have possibly heard a weak and injured old man yelling for help. His experiment showed that it just wasn't possible. He himself hadn't been able to make the boaters below hear him until he yelled as loud as he could, but Hum had said the rafters had said that someone had been yelling, "Help us," over and over.

He knew that sound carried differently depending on a number of conditions, which included wind and temperature and humidity, but he really didn't think the old man had it in him to yell that loud. After all, he had a severe head wound, and it was probable that someone in his shape wouldn't have been able to yell at all, yet alone over and over.

Now several people on a raft came floating down the river, and Bud repeated his experiment. They didn't hear him at all, and he guessed they must be talking to each other.

He tried one last time. "Helloooo!"

Someone answered back, but it wasn't anyone on the river, but rather someone standing right behind him, making Bud almost jump out of his skin.

"Well," Bud said, "I sure didn't hear you come up."

"That's because you were too busy making a racket," answered a short stocky man who reminded Bud a little of his Uncle Junior over in the Paradox Valley. A small two-door tan Jeep sat next to Bud's FJ.

The man held out his hand. "I'm Ryder Gates. You out here looking for Mackie's treasure, or you just seeing how loud you can yell?"

"No treasure," Bud replied, shaking the guy's hand. "But I actually was seeing if my voice would carry. I'm Bud Shumway. I live in Green River. Nice to meet you."

For some reason, Bud's intuition was telling him not to tell this particular guy much of anything, though he couldn't see any reason to be distrustful right off the bat.

Ryder said, "Well, I'm a hunter of types, and I'm definitely out here looking for Mackie's treasure. You know anything about it?"

Bud shook his head no. "About all I know is I've seen a lot of new people around this country lately. I suppose that's why, eh? But if I knew where his treasure was, I sure wouldn't be telling anybody."

"Well, that shows you're a smart man," Ryder said, smiling. "I've been looking for that treasure for 10 years, long before the old man published all that nonsense in that magazine and got everybody stirred up. Angus and I go way back, and he's a liar and a cheat."

Ryder obviously didn't know that Angus was dead, Bud noted, or else he was pretending he didn't. It surprised Bud that someone he barely knew would start bad-mouthing someone he didn't know at all. It seemed like bad form, though he was curious why Ryder would say such things about the old Scot.

"Well, I don't know," Bud replied. "But I better head back. My wife will be waiting for me."

Just then, he saw what looked to be Vern's plane rising from the distant haze, so he pointed and added, "That's her right there. I need to go now or she'll just keep on flying, and who knows where she'll land?"

Ryder grinned and said, "A pilot, is she? Well, there's a storm comin' in, so she better land soon. It was nice meeting you, Mr. Shumway, and I hope our paths cross again, but don't go yellin' like that just anywhere—they'll lock you up in the looney bin. I heard Angus was out in these parts, and if you run into him, tell him it's not nice to steal, and his old nemesis Ryder Gates is hot on his heels, as per usual."

"OK, but I doubt very much I'll run into him," Bud replied, frowning as he noted how quickly the clouds were building.

As he got into his FJ, he noticed Ryder had walked to the rim, where Bud thought he could hear him yelling out, "Helloooo down there!"

He shook his head, then headed back to the airport.

10

Bud sat in the back booth of the Melon Rind Cafe, drinking coffee and watching the rain wash the streaks of desert dust off the cafe windows.

It was a regular gully washer, which meant there was no need to do any irrigating that day. If it didn't let up soon, he figured he'd be out on Krider's farm trying to keep it from flooding.

He was hoping the storm would lift before long, as the sun would soon be at an angle that would make for a perfect rainbow. He could drive up Rooster Hill and get a great shot by the radio towers, but he then remembered that the road up the hill turned into gumbo when it was wet.

Noticing a big "For Sale" sign in the cafe window when he'd come in, Bud wondered how much business it had drummed up from locals wanting to know why Wilma Jean was selling it.

Even though he knew she'd just put the sign up that morning, Bud figured there were already a number of theories making the rounds, probably all the way from divorce and illness to winning the lottery, even though one had to drive 100 miles to Colorado to play. It wouldn't even surprise him if someone said it was because of all the spacemen everyone was seeing everywhere.

A booth up close to the front door held several guys who looked like they could be treasure hunters, and Bud wondered how one would tell the difference between a treasure hunter and a hiker. He knew that no sane hiker would be out in the summer heat, whereas treasure hunters weren't considered particularly sane to start with, so that wouldn't stop them.

He did know that the one thing that would stop everyone would be this storm, since most of the country around town was bentonite clay, which turned into slick grease when it got wet. He hoped Howie wasn't out in it.

Maureen came by and refilled Bud's coffee cup, and he asked if she knew where her husband was.

"I think he's down at the office," she replied. "You want a dab of vanilla ice cream with that?"

"Sure," Bud replied. "Actually, bring me a small dish. I can put some into my coffee and eat the rest. But say, Maureen, did he mention anything to you about an incident that made him need to get his headlight repaired?"

She laughed and sat down across from Bud, her red hair held back by a green paisley scarf.

"That guy," she began. "I love him dearly, but he's always coming up with something or other. He told me he pulled a man over last night for speeding, and when Howie asked the guy if he knew why he was pulling him over, he said, 'Because your patrol car headlight is out?' Can you imagine someone actually thinking something like that?"

She shook her head and hurried away as several people entered the cafe.

Bud thought back to when he'd been sheriff, and he knew Howie probably hadn't made the story up. He himself had encountered all kinds of crazy things when he'd been an LEO, including the night when a woman had flagged him down just to tell him he was good looking. Come to find out, one of the items on her bachelorette party treasure hunt was to flirt with a cop, and her friends had been watching from behind a nearby parked car.

He'd had other crazy things happen, including people wanting rides, asking if his badge was real, and being told by an offender that she had no right to be arrested by him. He'd had people say they didn't understand what he was saying, and had once intercepted a note between a guy driving without a license and his passenger that read, "Remember, I don't speak English and you're deaf."

Bud grinned to himself, then thanked Maureen as she returned, setting a small dish of ice cream in front of him.

"You're welcome," she replied, smiling. "By the way, Wilma Jean's at the bowling alley. She said to tell you she'll be there until closing. But the way you like ice cream, have you ever thought about getting your own ice-cream maker?"

Bud was genuinely surprised that the thought had never occurred to him, even though he knew she was just teasing. He told her he would look into it, as she went to wait on a man and woman who had just come in.

The couple didn't look at all like treasure hunters, Bud thought, deciding they must be tourists or someone passing through on their way to Salt Lake City or Denver, as they were dressed all in black.

He dropped a dollop of ice cream into his coffee and settled back, the rain still coming down hard. He would finish this cup, then go on home and say hello to the dogs, since it didn't look like the rain was going to let up soon.

He now took the small map from his shirt pocket and began copying it onto a napkin. He knew that Duncan would return for it at some point, and he wanted to have a copy for himself. He liked solving puzzles, though this one seemed unsolvable.

Done, he put the copy and the original both back into his pocket and pulled out the rock and started fiddling with it, wondering what or who had killed old Angus Mackie. The ambulance had taken the body up to the morgue in Price, where the coroner would hopefully shed some light on everything.

It sure seemed odd that he'd passed the Ford LTD while on his way out there—where had they been? There was really nothing out there for miles and miles. One would eventually reach Horseshoe

Canyon, which was becoming a tourist destination with its pictographs, but he couldn't picture them driving all the way out there in that car, as there were stretches of sand where they would definitely get stuck.

He fiddled more with the rock, turning it over and over, noting that it was beginning to take on a hint of rose color where his fiddling was starting to wear off the thin layer of travertine.

Must be rose quartz, he figured, wondering how long the rock had been at the geyser, sprayed daily with geyser water, travertine slowly accreting onto it. He knew that if he could somehow figure out what that accretion rate was, he would know how long the rock had been in the jar.

He now began wondering what Ryder had meant when he'd said he was Angus Mackie's nemesis. It seemed like a bad thing to say after Mackie had just been killed unless you wanted to be a murder suspect—or didn't know the old guy was dead.

Now Bud thought back to the map in his pocket and Duncan putting the key holder under his FJ. That in itself was odd, but its contents seemed even odder. And there sure seemed to be tumbleweeds everywhere lately, not only in real-life, but symbolizing something or other, though he had no idea what.

He thought again about what Angus Mackie had said just before he died—something that he wanted his grandson to know about a tumbleweed.

Bud sipped his coffee, thinking. What could the old guy have possibly meant? He'd said to tell his grandson that a tumbleweed is... no, wait, he hadn't said that at all, Bud mused.

The old guy hadn't said *a tumbleweed is*, but rather *tumbleweed is*, like it was a name. *Tumbleweed is*...Bud knew that a tumbleweed was a noxious invasive weed also known as Russian thistle that was brought into the West in stock feed back in the 1800s.

He was pretty sure that no one would want to relate this fact about tumbleweeds on their deathbed. Instead, most people, when dying, followed the tradition of relating something of great value to the living, something vitally important that must be told before you move on, hopefully to better things.

What Mackie had been trying to say had to be something important, Bud thought, but what was it? And who was his grandson? And what had he meant by a witch's tongue?

If Angus had indeed been in the LTD, maybe his grandson was the guy in the shades driving it, but then, why hadn't Angus just told the guy while they were in the car and before getting conked on the head or falling or whatever had happened? No, this elusive grandson had to be somewhere else, or Angus wouldn't have asked Bud to tell him.

Bud turned the rock around and around, rubbing its many facets. He thought back to his high-school grammar class, now getting himself even more confused.

He knew that a tumbleweed was a tumbleweed, but without the article "a," the word tumbleweed became more specific, referring to something maybe more like a town. It was kind of like saying a green river is a green river, but Green River is a town.

Angus had to be trying to tell his grandson that Tumbleweed was a place, not just a generic tumbleweed. That was the only way that what he said made any sense, at least to Bud.

Maybe Tumbleweed was one of the many railroad markers along the line through the Big Empty, like Sego and Desert and Solitude and Cedar and Stickers. He'd been in Tumbleweed, Arizona once, but that seemed unlikely.

Bud felt as if he'd made a breakthrough of some kind and yet was no further ahead in understanding anything than before. Yet if the Tumbleweed on the little map was an actual place, not a tumbleweed itself, maybe things would start to shape up, if he could figure out where that place actually was.

He put the rock back into his pocket and started drumming on the table when the cafe door opened and in walked someone he thought he recognized, even though they now looked like the proverbial drowned rat.

Duncan scanned the cafe as if looking for someone, and Bud

quickly realized he was that someone when Duncan made a beeline for his booth.

Leaning over Bud and dripping water onto the table, Duncan held up the key holder and quietly asked, "Where's my map? I know you have it. I need it back before someone else gets ahold of it."

11

"Have a seat," Bud said congenially. "You look like you could use a good cup of coffee, and maybe Maureen has a towel in the back you could borrow."

Duncan's wet clothes made a squishing noise as he slid into the booth, pulling his pack behind him, and Bud thought he looked even more bedraggled than when he'd first met him.

"I really need that map," Duncan said in a voice that Bud thought sounded kind of panicky.

"Well, as they say, possession's nine-tenths of the law," Bud replied.

"What do you mean by that?" Duncan asked with concern.

"It means I need something in exchange for hiding that map for you. We can do a trade—I'll give you the map back for a certain piece of information. But first, are you hungry?" He handed Duncan a menu. "On the house."

Duncan studied the menu for awhile, and Bud figured he must be hungry to forget the map even for a moment.

Finally, Duncan said, "A hamburger sounds really good, with fries. And maybe some of that hot tomato bisque soup and some rolls. And ice cream for dessert."

"A man after my own heart," Bud replied, waving to Maureen, who came and refilled Bud's coffee cup and took Duncan's order.

Duncan sighed. "This will be the first hot meal I've had in weeks." He turned around and scanned the cafe, pushing his wet hair away from his eyes, then asked, "What do you want for it?"

Bud took the map from his pocket and handed it to Duncan, saying, "I want to know why you hid it under my FJ. I know it's best to be a moving target, but how did you know you would ever get it back?"

Duncan again looked around the cafe furtively, put the map in the key holder, then said, "Because I know where you work. But you seem like a logical kind of guy. Why would anyone hide anything?"

"Because they're on foot and afraid they'll lose it?"

Duncan nodded as Maureen brought his food. "That's it exactly."

"You don't have a vehicle? How did you get to Green River?"

"I floated down."

"You floated down?"

"I hitched a ride with some rafters up at a put-in called Sand Wash, and we came through Desolation and Gray Canyons, so they said. It took five long days—five days of mosquitoes."

"Deso-Gray is a beautiful stretch of river," Bud said as Duncan stuffed a roll into his mouth. "Did you leave your car at Sand Wash?"

"No car," Duncan replied.

Bud sighed. "Someone's after you, aren't they? Is it someone in an old Ford LTD? You came down the river so they couldn't follow you, and that's why you hid the map under my FJ. You probably have it memorized anyway, but you want it back just in case. How do you know they won't take it from you now? They seem to have found out you're here."

"I'm going to hide it again," Duncan said. "I just needed to check something. How do you know all this?"

"Well, I didn't until just now when you said I did," Bud replied. "I was just guessing up until then."

Duncan looked at him with a mix of amusement and irritation.

"You should be a detective instead of a farmer. What's your name, anyway?"

"Bud Shumway."

"Well, Mr. Shumway, thanks for the lunch."

"You're welcome," Bud said. "But I have one more question, assuming you know the answer. What does the tumbleweed stand for?"

Duncan frowned. "You looked at the map."

"Just human curiosity."

"If I knew what it stood for, I wouldn't be sitting here, I'd be long gone. But why would I tell you, even if I knew?"

"No particular reason," Bud replied, "It's really none of my business."

Duncan studied him for awhile, finishing his hamburger and starting on the soup, then asked, "Have you lived here very long?"

"Quite awhile."

"Do you know the country around here?"

"Pretty well," Bud replied. "Are you looking for Mackie's treasure?"

Duncan looked long at Bud, then said, "I guess I might be."

"You're not sure?" Bud asked.

"OK, I'm sure, but why should I tell you anything?"

"You probably shouldn't," Bud said, "Since you don't know me from Adam. But are you using the poem? You do know that Mackie left a poem with clues?"

"I know. I'm not looking for *that* treasure."

"There's another one?" Bud asked, surprised. He waited, but Duncan said nothing, now seemingly preoccupied with his ice cream.

Bud was quiet for awhile, not sure if he should say anything, then finally asked, "Are you Angus Mackie's grandson?"

Duncan sat his spoon down slowly, reaching for his pack, then said, "Thanks again, but I need to go."

Bud wanted to tell Duncan his grandfather was dead and had left a message for him, but he also knew it was too early in the investigation to tell anyone. For all he knew, Duncan could've been involved in the murder, though Bud couldn't see the young man doing something like that. But he knew it was best not to say anything and let things shake out where they would.

Instead, he said, "Duncan, my wife and I have a trailer out at our place where you can stay if you need to. We don't live on the farm—we're closer to town, out on King's Lane. If you decide you want a place, nobody will know you're there but you and me and my wife."

Duncan, now standing, said, "That's really nice of you, Mr. Shumway. Not many people would offer a place to a complete stranger, especially one who looks like I do. But I can't tell you any more about the treasure than anyone else can."

"I'm not interested in the treasure," Bud replied. "I'm already a wealthy man. I would just prefer to not have to help the sheriff recover your body after you die of exposure."

"You're rich?" Duncan asked, looking suspicious.

"There are a lot of different types of wealth, Duncan. I may not be rich in money, but I have a lot of other things—my wife, my dogs, a comfortable house, a job I enjoy—well, you get the picture."

"I wish my grandfather was more like you," Duncan said, hoisting his pack over his back. "All his money won't do him much good now that he lives in a nursing home. Thanks again for the invite, I really do appreciate the offer."

With that, he turned and walked out the door. Bud watched out the window as Duncan walked around the corner then returned, again secretively slipping under the FJ, then disappearing into the rain.

Bud pulled the rock from his pocket and began fiddling with it, pondering the fact that, like Ryder, Duncan had talked about Angus as if he were still alive. He either didn't know the old man was dead or was pretending he didn't.

He then put the rock back into his pocket, left a tip for Maureen, and hurried to his FJ through the pouring rain. He wanted to go home for awhile and kick back, maybe read a good book or shop online for a new camera lens—do whatever it took to forget that he seemed to be getting involved in solving yet another murder, not to mention all the hubbub of Wilma Jean selling her businesses and learning to fly.

All he really wanted was to be a mellow melon farmer and live a life of peace and quiet.

12

Bud had spent the last hour or so looking online at lenses, Pierre in his lap and Hoppie at his feet. He was about ready to place his order when he decided he should give it a little time and let it rest for awhile.

No reason to get in a hurry, as it would probably be the only lens he'd be buying for awhile, given how expensive it was and their future financial state. He wanted to make sure it was what he really wanted.

He pushed back his recliner, his feet barely missing Hoppie's head, thinking again about Mackie's treasure and wondering what it was worth.

He sure would like to buy a new camera—one with higher resolution and a better sensor for taking night-sky photos. And he really wanted a new wide-angle lens, especially one of those new fast 24mm ones. His favorite night-sky photographer, Jennifer Wu, used one of those, and her photos were incredible.

Of course, he knew he'd have to improve his technical skills a lot before he could begin to take photos even close to hers. But maybe someday, if he could just afford some better equipment, he could become a Canon Master of Light, like she was. After all, he had won that ribbon at the fair up in Price with his train photo, so he must be on the right track.

Now something else crossed his mind, and he leaned forward and again picked up his laptop. He'd been wondering what the rate of accretion for travertine was, as it might give him an idea of how long the piece of quartz in his pocket had been subjected to geyser water.

He did a search, but most of the articles he found were way too technical with their deltas and psi's and differential equations, or at least that's what he thought they were. None were of much help, but he finally pulled one up about a place called Louie Creek in New Queensland, Australia, where it said that the accretion rate for travertine there was 4.15 mm per year.

He now did a search on millimeters, finding that one mm was about equivalent to the width of a coarse hair. Pulling the rock from his pocket, he held it up to the light, trying to gauge how thick the travertine was. It was impossible to tell just by looking, it was such a small amount.

He took a hair off Hoppie's back and held it up to the rock. It was just a guess, but the brown coating appeared to be about 10 hairs thick, which would mean it had been sitting in the jar for around 10 years, assuming the accretion rate was similar to the place in Australia.

As he held the quartz up, he was impressed at how sparkly it was where he'd rubbed off the travertine. He'd never seen such a deep ruby tint in a rose quartz, and it was almost dazzling when held up to the light. No wonder someone had faceted it, but why had they subjected it to the brown geyser water? It didn't make sense.

He now put the rock back into his pocket and did another Internet search, thinking of Maureen. He soon found an "Old-fashion, like grammar made, prime ice-cream mechanism with you crank handle only $49.99 free shipping, one bag salt, get started in finest craft of make own. Made in China."

He pressed the "One-Click Order" button on the screen and was promised that the ice-cream maker would arrive by Friday, though it didn't actually say *which* Friday.

Bud now wondered if the account was set up using his or Wilma Jean's debit card, as he couldn't remember. Oh well, he thought, if it was hers, he could just pay her back.

He then decided to do a search on Green River Spacemen, and found articles on spacemen and Green River, but nothing that included both. The spacemen articles looked interesting, but he decided he'd better not go down that rabbit hole or he might just disappear.

He'd gone down these holes before, sometimes taking hours before he found his way back up, and the funny thing about it, Bud mused, was that he usually couldn't even remember what he'd been doing all that time. It was kind of like having your car in park with the engine idling but no driver on board—your poor body sits there and waits for your mind to return, hoping it's not lost forever.

But wait, here was a recent comment on a popular site called Travel Advisor. Bud had seen the site before and thought it was very clever how its founders had created something with almost no content except what users would add.

The comment read:

Going to Green River is a trip back in time, and if you want to get scared to death, go up to the old missile base where we actually saw a spaceman. Nobody believes us, but we did, complete with white spacesuit. It even waved at us.

Bud grinned. Funny how the spacemen had studied human customs enough that they knew to wave at people.

The comment continued:

My boyfriend tried to take a photo, but by the time he got his phone out, it was gone. There's not much to do in the town unless you like to eat watermelons, but Crystal Geyser was nice, and there are supposed to be more small geysers around, which would be fun to find. We also liked the river history museum, and there's a really cute cafe there called the Melon

Rind that has to-die-for apple pie. Just stay away from that old missile base. —Rosebud

Bud wondered if Rosebud had tried the meatloaf at the cafe. That in itself would be worth a trip back to Green River, no matter where she was from.

He was tempted to leave a comment below hers, but he didn't want to have to register and go through all that, so he instead went back to looking at lenses again, putting one he wanted into the shopping cart. He sat there for awhile, then closed down the computer, wanting to think about it some more before spending his hard-earned cash.

His mind drifted back to the ice cream maker—now that would be something he could get into and enjoy. He'd better see if they had any frozen strawberries left from last summer in the freezer.

He lifted little Pierre from his lap and went into the kitchen, the dogs following along. Handing them each a Barkie Biscuit, he then opened the freezer door.

He was elated to find that there weren't just frozen strawberries inside, but also peaches and cherries from the orchards over in Palisade and Cedaredge in Colorado, where his wife and Maureen always made their annual pilgrimage to stock up. He also saw frozen pomegranate, but wasn't sure how that would taste in ice cream.

As he pulled out a carton of vanilla-bean ice cream, he wondered if Wilma Jean had been looking on the Internet for an airplane. Maybe he'd better order that lens while he could, because he had a feeling things were going to get pretty lean for awhile.

Sitting back down, he began eating straight from the carton, although feeling a bit guilty. Wilma Jean wasn't there to see him, so why did he feel that way, he wondered. He knew it must be because he'd already had ice cream at the cafe, and he'd promised her he'd try to stay away from sweets, seeing how his pants were getting a little tight around the waist.

He'd told her he was on a diet, and here he was ordering an ice-cream maker. He wondered if it was too late to cancel it, then decided it was, even though it had only been a few minutes.

Shoots, he thought, he would lose all those extra pounds as soon as the summer weeding season got into full swing, and after harvest time in the fall, he'd be skinnier than a toothpick. He would just tell her he was now on two diets, as the one diet didn't have enough food in it, and let it go at that.

He ate one last bite of ice cream, then put the carton back, thinking the few spoonfuls he'd eaten didn't really amount to much.

As he walked back into the living room, he could see the rain had finally stopped, and the sun was trying to break free from the clouds. He grabbed his camera and went outside, dogs following, where he looked in the direction he knew a rainbow might appear.

But instead of seeing a rainbow, he saw, standing right there on the other side of the fence in broad daylight, a spaceman in a brilliant white suit, who appeared to be trying to pull his big heavy feet from the mud.

Hoppie and Pierre started barking their little heads off, and Bud thought he could make out muffled metallic noises through the helmet, though he had no idea what they could mean.

All he knew was that a spaceman was standing by his back fence, gesticulating and making strange sounds, and he wasn't sure what it might do to the dogs, yet alone him.

13

Bud stood frozen for a moment, not sure what to do, when it finally occurred to him that the dogs weren't a bit afraid.

If it were a real spaceman, he thought, surely the dogs would at the very least know something was seriously wrong and want back inside.

Instead, Pierre, in true dachshund style, had his head under the fence and was biting at the being's white puffy suit legs, grabbing ahold of the nearest one and chewing on it. The being tried to kick him away, but his feet were stuck in deep gumbo and he couldn't move in the cumbersome suit.

Wilma Jean was right, Bud thought, he needed to plant something in that strip between the lawn and the barn. He'd have to get Krider's tractor over here one of these days and put in some nice alfalfa for the wild rabbits—that would keep Hoppie and Pierre entertained, for sure.

"Seems like someone didn't do their research," Bud said. "They need to design you guys a better suit. You can't begin to withstand the hazards of a dangerous planet like Earth if you can get stuck in just a little gumbo."

The spaceman made a lot of metallic noises, but Bud couldn't understand anything, so he went over to the fence, reaching over and helping pull him out of the mud. The suit crinkled like paper where he pulled until part of one sleeve came completely off. Beneath was an arm that looked suspiciously human.

"For crying out loud, help me get this stupid helmet off," said the metallic voice.

"Righty tighty, lefty loosey?" Bud asked, trying to unscrew the helmet as Pierre still chewed on the suit leg, part of it now almost stripped off.

"Climb over the fence," Bud said. "I can't get to you."

He helped pull the being over into the yard, where Hoppie now started helping Pierre chew on the other pant leg.

Bud called them off, and they were so excited that they began running in circles on the grass, chasing each other and barking.

"They don't get to attack spacemen very often," Bud explained. "Talk about the ultimate bragging rights—way better than a postman. Here, let me try it now."

Bud soon had the helmet off, revealing a middle-aged man with red matted hair and sweat running down his face.

"No climate control?" Bud asked. "How did you guys even make it here alive?"

"OK, OK," said the guy. "I guess you deserve to have fun at my expense, but man, show some pity. This is a tough job."

"If you guys have to invade in the summer, you should at least be smart enough to go to Alaska instead of the Utah desert," Bud replied. "And I would also think you would know that hotdogs are bad for you. Just think of what's in them."

"Hotdogs?" asked the man.

"I heard that two spacemen were down by the river roasting hotdogs," Bud replied.

The guy laughed. "That would be Kenny and Joe. They're idiots."

The man now began peeling off the rest of the suit, which appeared to be made mostly of something that looked like crepe paper, while Hoppie and Pierre watched to see if he needed help. Underneath, he was dressed in what looked to be standard camouflage army shirt and pants, his clothes almost as soaked as if he'd been swimming.

"You have anything cold to drink?" he asked.

"Come on in the house," Bud replied. "You might want to take your boots off, though, so my wife won't get upset."

"I don't think I can," the man replied. "Can you just bring it out here?"

"You want some vanilla ice cream with that?" Bud asked.

The man nodded his head yes, and Bud quickly returned with a large glass of cold lemonade and a dish of ice cream. The man quickly drained the glass, then started on the ice cream.

"You sure these Earth foods won't harm you?" Bud grinned. "I wouldn't want anything to do with that. We need to be on peaceful terms with you and your leaders. Or maybe you are the leader? Tell your fellow beings that Bud Shumway says you're welcome here on Planet Earth as long as you don't try to steal our minerals."

"Thanks," the man said, extending his hand. "I'm Lieutenant Walter Esker—you can call me Walt. I was trying to get a drink from your hose. Sorry for the intrusion."

Bud nodded, and the man continued, "Say, I would really appreciate it if you wouldn't tell anyone about this. I'm on a top secret mission with the Army. Seems that a number of aliens have been sighted around here, and I'm part of a group sent to check it out. We don't want to worry anyone."

"You mean spacemen, not aliens," Bud corrected him.

"You're right, spacemen. I didn't know there was a difference."

"Is that why you're in disguise, to try and sneak up on them?"

The man looked embarrassed. "Yes, I told them it was a dumb idea, well, as much as you can tell top brass something like that, but they wouldn't listen. But would you mind giving me a ride?"

"Where to?" Bud asked.

"Back out to the old missile base. That's where we're headquartered. We have a couple of camp trailers we brought in. I need to reconnoiter, get a new spacesuit."

"Sure," Bud replied. "Though it's amazing how quickly you adapted to our environment without one. But I have a favor to ask."

"What's that?" Walt asked, handing Bud the glass and ice-cream dish.

"If we see the sheriff, I'd like you to put your helmet back on for a minute and wave. Just a little joke on him, of course," Bud replied. "He's a good friend."

"I normally couldn't say yes to something like that," Walt replied. "But since you've been such a help, just give the word."

Bud grinned as he helped Lieutenant Walter Esker load what was left of his suit into the FJ, then put the dogs in the back and headed out.

It had been fun, but he had a feeling that there was something Walt wasn't telling him, something that could turn out to be important to the people of Green River.

14

"Sheriff, I'm the sheriff, and you're obligated by law to tell me anything you might know that could help me do my job of protecting the American public," Howie advised Bud, studying his face as he stood by the FJ's window, the patrol vehicle parked behind, lights flashing.

Bud saw Old Man Green and Junkyard Goldie drive by in Old Man Green's pickup, slowing and looking for a minute like they would stop, though they didn't.

Howie continued. "I know what I saw—you had a spaceman in your FJ. I don't care how casually you waved at me and pretended everything was normal, I saw it with my own two eyes. If you don't tell me what's going on, I'm going to have to assume you've been brainwashed by them and act accordingly."

"What will you do?" Bud asked, grinning.

Howie pleaded, "Sheriff, I might just have to lock you up for your own safety. We don't want to go there, now, do we? We're friends."

Bud replied, "No, especially since the jail's a few hours away over in Castle Dale. You'll miss band practice. Isn't this Wednesday?"

Howie leaned back for a moment, frustrated, nodding his head at a car of tourists driving slowly by, gawking.

"Did they ask you to do anything suspicious? Let me look in your eyes." Howie shone his big flashlight in Bud's eyes as Bud blinked and turned away.

"They wanted me to take a survey," Bud replied.

"A survey? Seriously? What did it ask?"

"It asked if I believed in spacemen," Bud grinned. "Look, Howie, I promised I wouldn't tell anyone, but I will say it wasn't a real spaceman. Let me just say the military's doing some research, just as I thought. It's nothing to worry about."

"Where were you taking him?"

"Out to the missile base. The guy came to the house looking for water. He got hot in that suit, but he wasn't a real spaceman, not the kind from another world, unless you think the military's another world, which it probably is. I asked him to put his helmet on if we saw you as a little joke."

Howie now came around to the passenger side and got into the FJ with a sigh of relief.

"Bud, you know I would never throw you in jail, well, not unless you did something really bad, anyway. Thanks for telling me that. I won't repeat it to anyone. Did he say what kind of research they're doing?"

"Not really," Bud answered.

"Well, I have a theory on that," Howie replied. "I think they're here testing the proton pulse. It's the perfect place for it, as they already have a base established and the night sky is so clear and we're not around any urban areas."

"What in hellsbells is the proton pulse?" Bud asked as a black Mustang with California plates came roaring up, screeching to a crawl upon seeing the patrol car.

"Well, it's like this," Howie replied, nodding his head congenially at the speeders in the Mustang. "Every once in awhile the hydrogen atoms in the atmosphere build up enough that they have to release, and when they do, the whole atmosphere pulses for a microsecond. It's so fast we humans don't see it."

"Then how do we know about it? Who discovered it?"

"I'm not sure, but it was probably through some scientific error, you know, looking for something else with some kind of high-tech instrument," Howie replied.

A school bus stopped right in front of the FJ and several kids got out, waving at Bud and Howie, then ran across the road to several houses.

"How do you know about it?" Bud asked.

"Some guy at the astronomy club meeting up in Price told me about it. Say, there's that little boy who broke the window over at the hardware store last year," he noted. "He sure got in a lot of trouble, but he seems to have straightened out. Had to work there after school till it was paid for, and now he has a regular part-time job there."

"That's Susan Pratt's boy," Bud said. "She works over at the grocery store. His dad's gone all the time up to Price working in the coal mine. But Howie, I need to go. Have you heard anything back from the coroner about Angus Mackie yet?"

"I have, Bud."

Bud waited as Howie watched the kids, who were now playing a game of soccer with a rock.

It now seemed to Bud that the good old days were back, when Howie was his deputy and always saved the important news for last, making Bud feel like he was pulling teeth to get any information.

"What did he say?" Bud asked patiently.

"Who say?" asked Howie.

"The coroner."

"Sorry, Bud, I was thinking about that spaceman. The coroner said Mackie died from severe head trauma. He couldn't tell if it was from being hit or if he'd fallen, but he said it was pretty bad and he'd have to have fallen pretty hard to do it."

Bud suddenly had a sinking feeling that he might not ever know if Mackie was actually murdered or not. Part of the reason Bud had been such a good sheriff was that he hated open loops, not knowing what and why something had happened, and this news bothered him. He liked closure, and he was feeling like he might not get it in this case.

"That's it?" Bud asked.

"That's it," Howie replied. "I don't know whether to close the case or not, Bud. Seems like we have no evidence that it was murder at this point."

Bud said, "Agree, but don't close it just yet, Sheriff. We need more time to figure out what he was doing out there and who knew about it, if anyone."

"I agree," Howie replied. "I've been trying to find his next of kin. The coroner said the body definitely is Angus Mackie—I guess he checked his dental records. His next of kin is his grandson, Duncan Mackie, but it appears that his nephew, Graham Mackie, has power of attorney over his affairs. Graham's wife is named Clara."

Bud asked, "Have you been able to notify them about his remains?"

"No, not yet. I contacted the sheriff where they live down in St. George, and he hasn't been able to find anyone at home."

"That may be because they're up here," Bud said, thinking of the Ford LTD.

"How do you know that?"

"I'm just guessing. I think it may be the couple in the Ford LTD, but like I said, it's just a guess. I have nothing to base it on."

"Oh, hey, Sheriff, that reminds me. I got a call from Joe Nelson, and he said there's a tent out by his gravel pit that appears to be abandoned. He goes out there several times a day and hasn't seen anyone around. Thought we might want to go check it out. Where is his pit exactly?"

Bud replied, "It's not far from where we found Angus. Instead of taking the road to Lover's Leap, keep going on down the hill and take a left just past where that old rusted car is, then go down towards the river. It's just across from Crystal Geyser. It'll be too muddy to go out there for awhile. But Howie, isn't that your radio squawking?"

Howie jumped out and ran to the Land Cruiser, then was soon back at Bud's window.

"Glad you heard that. It was the State Patrol. They need a wide-load escort through town."

"Why are they stopping in Green River and not just staying on the freeway?" Bud asked.

"They're bringing in some kind of an airplane and taking it out to the airport. I guess the wide load is the fuselage, and the wings are on a separate truck. You don't suppose this has anything to do with your wife, do you, Sheriff?"

Howie turned and got into his patrol vehicle, taking off towards the freeway, siren blasting and lights on, leaving Bud to ponder the news that a plane was coming into Green River on a big flatbed truck.

15

"I bought it on eBay," Wilma Jean said, and Bud thought he could see the look of excitement on her face, even though she was down at the bowling alley and he still sat in his FJ where Howie had pulled him over.

It was just like his wife to not waste time when she decided to do something, so Bud wasn't a bit surprised to find out the plane was hers.

Wilma Jean said, "Hellooo. You still there, hon?"

"Just trying to process what you just said," he replied. "You actually bought an airplane on eBay?"

"No, no, I'm sorry, hon. That was supposed to be a little joke. Actually, what it was, well, I was testing you to see how you would react if I really *did* buy a plane on eBay—I have been looking there some. It's actually Vern's, a plane he got a few months ago that needs some work. Since there's no hanger at Hanksville, he's renting space in the airport hanger here and the airport mechanic—you remember Sammy—is going to get it all shipshape. That's why it's coming in on a flatbed truck—it's not airworthy."

Bud sighed. "Shoots. I was getting kind of excited there for a minute, thinking you had a plane."

"Well, I actually might. Once it's fixed up, I'm thinking of buying it from Vern. That's part of the reason he's getting it fixed. He's been putting it off, not wanting to spend the money, thinking he'd do it himself, but he's too busy."

"Did *he* buy it off eBay?" Bud asked.

"No, it's from some guy he met out in the desert. They had to take off the wings and disconnect the sensitive electronics and wrap it to make sure no water could get into the engine or anything, especially with all this rain, before they could haul it. Do you see it coming yet?"

"No," Bud replied. "But I hear it."

"Hear it?"

"Yeah, Howie's escorting it with his siren on. What kind of plane is it? Wait, I can see something coming now. They just passed the Westwind."

"Follow it out to the airport and see if you can get some good pictures, hon. It's a Piper Cub. I wish I could go. Trying to operate this darn bowling alley all by myself is running me ragged," she said.

"I can come down if you want," Bud replied. "I'm not doing much. The fields are too wet."

"It's OK, hon. I may be able to get one of my temps to come in and spell me for awhile. You go on out and check out that airplane for me."

Bud could now see the entourage, a big flatbed truck holding the fuselage of a plane, and behind that, another truck carrying the wings, everything wrapped with tarps and cloth to keep out moisture.

They slowly came up Main Street and crossed the river, then turned left down Green River Boulevard and went by the golf course, then by Howie and Maureen's big farm house. The trucks were soon carefully crossing the tracks and heading on out to the airport, and it sounded like Howie had finally turned off his siren, now that they were out of town.

"So far, so good," Bud thought, following along. The entourage reached the intersection with the River Road and turned right towards the airport.

As Bud came to the intersection, he pulled over, getting out of the

FJ so he could take some good photos of the entourage with the San Rafael Reef in the background. He knew that the jagged teeth of the rugged uplift would make quite a scenic photo.

He now watched as two figures came into view in the distance on the River Road, and it made him think of when he'd first seen Duncan. It was probably someone who'd managed to get themselves stuck, and since it was a few miles into town, he decided to wait and see if they needed help.

He watched as the figures slogged through the mud, gradually getting closer, wondering why anyone would be out in that country in such wet weather.

Finally, as they came closer, he was surprised to see the couple from the Ford LTD. They were soaking wet with gumbo splattered up to their knees, and both looked exhausted.

"Say, would you mind giving us a ride into town?" asked the man, no longer wearing the reflective sunglasses. "We got ourselves a little stuck out there. We've only walked a couple of miles, though it seems like a hundred in this mud."

"What happened?" Bud asked.

"Well, like I said, we got stuck," the man answered. "We're camping out there and had no idea it could get muddy like this."

"*He* had no idea, he should say," the woman said with disgust. "I told him the sign said impossible when wet, and he chose to ignore both me and the sign."

"*Impassible* when wet, Clara, and you have a right to be miffed, but we don't need to air our laundry in front of this gentleman," the man said apologetically. "I had no idea that mud like this even existed. I'm Graham Mackie and this is my wife Clara. We're from St. George, and it's sandy down there. You don't get stuck like this when it rains. This is just terrible." He tried to kick the mud off his feet as he talked, to little avail.

Bud immediately thought of the tent Joe Nelson had reported, and asked, "Are you tent camping down by the river across from the geyser?"

"That's us," Clara answered wryly. "We have a perfectly nice home at home, but we had to come up here to see what it's like to make fools of ourselves. I already knew Graham was a fool, but I underestimated myself." She still had her hair done up in the blue curlers, and Bud noted that it would be a good way to keep one's hair under control when camping.

"Are you treasure hunting like everyone else out here?" Bud asked.

Graham and Clara exchanged glances, and Bud suddenly got the feeling they didn't want to say more.

Finally, Graham said, "We are treasure hunting of a sort, though actually, we're looking for my uncle. Has anyone by chance reported an elderly white-haired gent wandering around anywhere? He's 85, and we're getting desperately worried. That's why we decided to walk into town instead of waiting for the mud to dry up—heaven only knows how long that will take."

Bud sighed. He knew he was talking to the nephew of Angus Mackie, but he had no intention of telling him Angus was dead, at least not until he and Howie could properly interrogate the couple.

"How long has he been missing?" Bud asked.

"Since yesterday evening," Clara answered. "He used to be a uranium prospector out here a long time ago, and he wanted us to bring him out to reminisce about the good old days."

Graham interrupted, "He has sundowner's syndrome. Are you familiar with that?"

"Not really," Bud replied. "Is that where you get restless at sundown and want to flee?"

"Yes, exactly," said Clara. "It's somewhat common among old people, and no one knows why. It's a real problem for nursing homes, as the oldsters try to escape, even though they have no idea where they're escaping to."

"He took off after dinner and disappeared. We called and called for him, but couldn't find hide nor hair," Graham said.

"I told Graham that Uncle Angus would never find his way back,"

Clara added. "But no point arguing. Living with a couple of Scots hasn't been easy, you know. Graham and Angus have made me realize that the old saw is true—it's necessary to either kill a Scot or agree with him, you have no other choice."

"He used to be quite independent and self-sufficient," Graham added, ignoring his wife. "I told him over and over not to go out on his own. I really did think he would come back. We finally drove into town and tried to get the sheriff, but couldn't find him, so we went back out. We looked for him almost all night, calling and calling, as much as we could. And when I finally agreed with Clara that we should go for help again, it was too late."

"How so?" Bud asked, thinking of the old guy on the ground, Howie's coat covering him.

"It started raining and was too muddy to get out," Clara said. "And by then, our cell phone battery was dead."

Bud sighed, then said, "Well, climb on in. I'll take you to the Robber's Roost Motel. It's very reasonable, and the grocery store's nearby, as well as a nice little cafe. You can wait out the mud there, and when it's dried up, either me or the sheriff can bring you back out to your car and help you get it unstuck."

"What about our shoes?" Clara asked. "I don't want to get your vehicle all muddy."

"It's OK," Bud replied, putting the dogs into the front with him. "It won't be the first or last time. Hop on in."

Bud turned the FJ back towards Green River, hoping that if he hurried and got them settled in he could get back out to the airport before they unloaded the plane and get more photos for Wilma Jean.

He knew he should try to get more information from Graham and Clara, but he was beginning to feel somewhat disheartened by the whole situation, and besides, he wasn't even sure at this point that Angus had actually been murdered. It seemed that everyone who could possibly be a suspect thought he was still alive.

Back in town at the motel, Graham asked, "Do you know how we can reach the sheriff? We need to get in touch with him and get a search effort going for my uncle."

Bud again hesitated, wanting to tell them their uncle was dead. Instead, he said, "I'm on my way to see the sheriff right now, and I'll tell him. Do you have a contact number where he can reach you?"

"Well, yes, except my phone's dead," Graham replied. "Have him call us here at our room."

"That'll work," Bud said.

Now Graham turned and came back to the FJ window as Clara went on into the office. "Say," he said. "I never even thanked you or got your name."

"Bud Shumway. I used to be the sheriff here. We'll be talking again, I'm sure."

"Oh, I hope so, Bud," Graham said congenially. "But do you think I could borrow enough cash to get us through until we get back to our car? We left everything there."

Bud pulled out some cash and handed it to Graham, who thanked him profusely and went into the motel office.

With that, Bud was soon heading back in the direction of the airport. He had just crossed the railroad tracks and pulled over to call Howie when Wilma Jean went around him in her big pink Mary Kay Lincoln Continental, honking and waving. She appeared to be going out there herself, and Bud figured she'd found someone to cover for her at the bowling alley.

He waved, barely registering it was her, as he was thinking about what Clara had said about it being necessary to either kill a Scot or agree with them.

Had they killed Angus? If so, it was unlikely she would say something like that. Like Duncan and Ryder, she and Graham both spoke as if the old man were still alive. It was a conundrum, for sure, he thought, turning back towards town.

Howie still wasn't answering his phone. He was probably too busy helping them unload the plane, Bud figured.

The stress of trying to figure out what had happened to Angus Mackie was wearing on him, and Bud knew he badly needed to get away. The farm would wait, as there would be no need to irrigate after the big rain, and Wilma Jean wouldn't miss him if he took off for a couple of days, especially with all the excitement of a new airplane.

Bud knew exactly who could help him find the peace and quiet he needed—a man who knew every square inch of the Big Empty like the back of his hand and who disappeared in it every chance he got, a man with the name of Eldon Daddage.

16

Bud felt a sense of relief wash over him as he hung up the phone after talking to Eldon, as he knew getting away was just what he needed.

Eldon was the founder of the BOB-O, or Bucket of Bolts Overlanders, and he and a friend had an outing planned that very day, which Eldon said Bud was more than welcome to join. They were going out to reconnoiter a route down to June's Bottom for the club's annual outing, making sure the trail was still passable, as no one had been down it for some time.

June's Bottom was a river bottom where the legendary June Marsing and his family had weathered out the Great Depression on a small farm, growing melons and produce in the rich soils along the Green from the mid to late 1930s.

June was reported to be the finest roper that had ever ridden the desert, and he'd later built the small motel and gas station that had serviced the uranium miners at Temple Junction between Green River and Hanksville. Bud had heard somewhere that June was related to the flying Wells family, maybe by marriage, and he wondered if June had ever flown with Gas.

Along with June's Bottom, there were lots of river bottoms along the Green, places where boaters now camped under big cottonwoods, most named after whoever had farmed them or run stock there, though some of the bottoms were inaccessible from above because of huge cliffs.

Besides June's Bottom, Bud knew of Anvil Bottom, Cabin Bottom (named for an old cabin that had burned down), Anderson Bottom, Harris Bottom, Bull Bottom (where the pioneer Chaffin family had ranged their bulls), and Mineral Bottom.

There was also a Spanish Bottom, the origin of its name lost in the annals of time, though some thought it had been named for Spanish gold seekers of long ago. And sometimes the names got a bit humorous—Bud's favorite was Fuller Bottom, although it was on the San Rafael River and not the Green.

Once on the river bottom, the club would eat too much and tell lies over a campfire after exploring the old ruins along the river, assuming anything was left of the old corral and stone house.

Bud had only been down the trail once, and he remembered that it had indeed been a difficult route to find. The actual route wasn't as scary as it looked from the rim, but it was tricky enough that one wanted to know more than a little about how their rig handled on the grippy sandstone, as well as how to navigate tippy rocks.

Once down, Bud still recalled how surprised some passing rafters had looked as he sat on the bank of the river, and a couple had even stopped to ask him if he were stuck and needed a ride, thinking he'd somehow lost his boat. They were even more surprised when they saw Bud's FJ at the bottom of the steep cliffs.

Bud was excited to be going back, looking forward to a couple of days out under the sun and stars, even though the dogs looked dejected when he told them they couldn't go.

It was just too hot, and he worried about them being around sheer cliffs. He also didn't want them around the deep river, as the Green was running bank full.

Bud began whistling as he packed his gear. He wouldn't really need much for just a couple of days, but he wanted to be sure he had both the cool nights and hot days covered.

As he took his khaki shirt from the wash, he realized with a sinking feeling that he'd forgotten all about the rose quartz and left it in his pocket. He held the shirt up, noting that the rock appeared to have worn a hole, and Bud was relieved to find it was still in the washing machine, no worse for the wear. He was surprised, as he'd left a gazillion rocks in his pockets before and none had torn a hole through a cotton shirt like that.

He again held the quartz up to the light, noting that even more of the travertine was gone. It shone like a jewel, reflecting a ruby-colored light on the beige wall, which Hoppie started biting at while Pierre barked.

Sticking the rock back into his pocket, Bud went into the kitchen, gave the dogs each their obligatory Barkie Biscuit, then rifled through the cupboards looking for the kind of food that could survive not being refrigerated for a few days.

He found a couple of cans of black olives, some cereal, canned milk that he knew Wilma Jean kept for cooking, and various assorted cans of vegetables and beans. He figured he could stop at the grocery store on his way to meet up with Eldon and get a few more things, maybe even some fresh foods if Eldon had room in his cooler, as well as a supply of Old Man Green's watermelon spritzer.

Bud had a nice cooler, but he wouldn't be allowed to bring it, as the rules for the Bucket of Bolts Overlanders stated that one could only use equipment that was at least 25 years old, and his cooler was much newer than that. He was lucky that his FJ qualified, as the rules also applied to vehicles, and one couldn't drive anything worth more than $3,000.

Bud and Eldon both knew that his FJ, as well as some of the other rigs the members had, were verging on being collectibles and potentially worth much more, but that was something they couldn't control, so it was generally ignored.

But everything, all the gear, had to be older, and one was encouraged to bring things like old coffee percolator pots, canvas water bags that hung off your antenna, and kerosene Coleman lanterns with the original-style wicks. Cell phones had to be kept turned off, and GPS's weren't allowed, only maps.

It was also expected that one would wear old clothes, and Bud had found that the Green River Thrift Store was a good place to find what you needed along those lines, unless you knew one of the old missile base guys was having a yard sale.

The general idea, according to the BOB-O brochure that Eldon had made up, was to try to recreate the good old days before everyone spent their time in their tents watching DVDs. Of course, Bud knew that was in itself old school, as now everyone could just stream videos off the Internet if they had a smartphone, but he didn't say anything, not wanting to make Eldon think he needed to update his brochure.

Bud wondered what the indigenous people would have thought about it all, and he often reminded Eldon that in order to be technically correct on this good old days thing they'd have to go on foot, eat rabbits, and wear loincloths, but Eldon always said that was *way way* before the good old days.

Bud next called Wilma Jean and told her about the trip, but she seemed distracted, excited about the airplane. Since Howie was still out at the airport helping supervise the unloading of the plane, she promised to tell him about the couple at the motel.

Bud was glad Wilma Jean was distracted, as she wouldn't be wishing he was around to help out, though she was generally pretty understanding about his need to escape into the backcountry once in awhile.

Almost done, Bud carried his gear out to the FJ, being sure he had his camera and tripod, as he knew the night sky would be stunning way out there. He knew Eldon would disapprove, since his camera wasn't 25 years old, but he also knew they would like seeing photos of themselves, and since it was a recon trip, he knew they could bend the rules a bit. He could maybe even try some light painting on the canyon walls with his old Ray-O-Vac flashlight, making the sandstone glow beneath the starry sky.

Back inside, he filled his old vintage Thermos with coffee, added a dollop of ice cream, patted the dogs on the head and gave them each another biscuit, then headed out the door, wearing an old straw hat with vintage fishing flies stuck in the brim, orange plaid pants, and a worn blue Levi's shirt with mother of pearl buttons, the rose quartz secure in its front pocket.

17

"You look pretty silly," Eldon told Bud with approval as they walked around the grocery store, stocking up on supplies.

"Thanks," Bud grinned, as a pair of mountain bikers in sleek lycra pants and shirts watched them with amusement, trying not to be obvious.

Eldon was dressed in a tan polyester stretch leisure suit that made him look like he either just came from the lounge at the old defunct Country Club Nightclub or was getting ready to crawl under a car with a wrench.

Eldon's best friend, Frosty Merriott, who was joining them on the recon, had found an old pair of bell-bottom jeans from somewhere and topped it with a t-shirt with the words, "KOAL, Voice of Castle Country, Price, Utah." Over this he wore a black velvet-rope bolo tie with an alabaster clasp turning yellow with age.

Susan Pratt, the mother of the boy Bud and Howie had watched get off the bus, checked them out, smiling.

"Looks like the relics are out and about," she joked. "Or should I call you the remnants? Where you guys going this time?"

"We're going down to June's Bottom," Eldon replied, paying with his smartphone as Susan ran his groceries through the checkout.

Everyone in Green River knew about the BOB-O's, and probably half the residents had been on at least one expedition through the years. A lot of them would loan out gear to friends and family who wanted to go.

Susan replied, "You guys are going to have a great time. If you meet a stranger, you can tell them they accidentally travelled back in time, and they'll believe you."

"Until Bud starts talking about some shade-grown organic gourmet coffee," Eldon said. "All they had back in the good old days was Arbuckles. Say, Bud, did you bring some ice cream? You can put it in my cooler."

Bud replied, "No, but did I tell you I ordered an ice-cream maker? It's an old-fashioned hand-crank type, so I'll be able to bring it next time and we can make ice cream out in the middle of nowhere."

They were soon outside, putting the groceries into their vehicles, when the two mountain bikers came up to them.

"Say, we overheard you guys talking about going to June's Bottom. There's supposed to be a mountain bike route down in there. Do you know anything about it?"

"No, never heard of it," Eldon replied.

"Would you mind if we followed you out there? We're from Salt Lake and usually go down to Radium to bike, but someone told us about this place."

"You mean follow us all the way down to the river, or just to the rim?" Eldon asked.

"Well," the young man said, "Probably just to the rim, though if you could show us the route down, that would be great, too."

"You guys are too contemporary to hang with us," Eldon said gruffly, pointing to the vanity plate on his old Willy's Jeep that read, "BOB-O."

"Are you Bob?" the man asked, confused.

"No, that stands for Bucket of Bolts Overlanders. You have to have equipment a lot older than you guys put together to come along. And look at the way you're dressed, totally unsuitable to hang with us."

"Now Eldon," Frosty intervened. "Don't be a snob like that.

Remember the whole reason of the BOB-O's is to help people remember the joys of the good old days. Guys like this are the very reason you started this thing."

"Not necessarily," Eldon replied. "You have to have been a part of the good old days to remember them. These guys are too young."

"That's not true at all," Frosty said. "Every trip we've had there have been kids along. It's important to show them a better way to live."

"A better way?" asked the biker, even more confused.

"Are you willing to give up your electronic toys if you come with us?" Eldon asked.

"Toys?"

"You know, like your cell phone and GPS and DVD player."

"DVD player?" The other biker asked, puzzled.

"OK, whatever. Seems like you're not." Eldon said abruptly.

Now Bud intervened. "Eldon, even if they're not up to BOB-O standards, I vote we let them come along. What happened to your Western hospitality? We might learn a thing or two from them, and we sure don't have a corner on the canyons. Besides, I've always wanted to try one of those fat-tired bikes." He pointed to the two bikes on their nearby 4Runner.

"We just want you to show us the route down," the biker said. "We're not expecting you to entertain and feed us."

"You don't understand," Frosty said. "Showing you the route down is no minor thing. You'll have to follow along with us, think like us, become one with us." He now started making sounds like an alien, twirling his fingers over his head like antennae.

Bud quickly interrupted, "Look, fellows, you don't know Frosty, he has a weird sense of humor, and we've been having a few strange sightings going on around here."

He paused, wondering for a moment what Howie was doing, then continued. "Actually, that in itself is a good reason for us all to stick together, and we can always use another more reliable vehicle, seeing how ours are all buckets of bolts. I think you should come along. It's not really a route one should go on alone in case you have problems, like a broken axle."

The two bikers looked at each other, then shook their heads in agreement.

"We really would enjoy learning more about the good old days," one said. "Especially if it means we can find the route down to June's Bottom."

"We're going over to the Westwind to gas up," Bud said. "We'll meet you over there."

"And hopefully, you have some more appropriate clothes to put on," Eldon added, handing them a BOB-O brochure.

18

Bud stood on the rim far above the Green River, colorful agatized rocks littering the ground. The river sure lived up to its name with its green hue, he thought.

He knew it was a good thousand feet down to the big Fremont cottonwoods lining the waterway and providing shelter and respite from the heat to the many species of birds and wildlife.

He'd even seen beaver down on some of these river bottoms, though he knew they preferred smaller streams where they could build their dams.

He could now see a small white V on the water, and as it moved along, he knew it was the wake of one of the jetboats owned by Green River Waterways, a local boating company who supplied raft and canoe rentals and river shuttles.

He wondered where it was going, then noted it stopped just below him along the far side of the river. It wasn't long until it was moving again, now going back upriver, and he wondered if it might be treasure hunters.

It hadn't been long since the annual Green River Friendship Cruise on Memorial Day. He and Wilma Jean often went along as a sweep boat, but they were too tired this year from their Montana vacation and had missed it.

Bud could see June's Bottom far below, and it seemed unlikely they would ever make it down there alive. He thought of Angus Mackie, wondering if the old guy had stood on the rim upriver before he'd died, looking down below, enjoying the view like Bud was, no idea he would soon be gone.

Bud wondered why Graham and Clara had been out tent camping with an old guy in his 80's, especially if he was prone to wander off in the evenings. Why not at least get a nice motel room where they could all be safe and comfortable?

Neither of the pair looked like the camping type, and their old LTD certainly wasn't suited to any kind of backcountry travel, as they'd found out.

Bud was standing a good 10 feet from the edge of the cliff, but it still felt heady and like he could just tip over and fall off. He'd never liked heights and figured he was prone to a bit of vertigo. He hoped Wilma Jean wouldn't ask him to fly with her, at least not often, though he figured he could probably handle it once or twice.

He recalled how Angus had been by the rim when they'd found him, way too close to the edge. One thing that had struck Bud as odd was the fact that Angus had fallen with his back to the cliff, which meant he had either turned before he fell or was walking away from the edge. Maybe someone had hit him and he'd turned to see who it was before collapsing.

Now Bud thought of Duncan and wondered if he'd managed to figure out what the word tumbleweed was all about. He then wondered about Duncan floating down the river from Sand Wash and how he didn't have a car. How had he gotten to Sand Wash to hitch a ride in the first place? It was way off the beaten path, though maybe he'd hitched a ride there, too. And why go to all that trouble of spending almost a week rafting to get to Green River? He'd acted like he didn't want to tell Bud anything. Was there a reason, or was Bud just being overly suspicious?

He now looked back to where Frosty, Eldon, and the two bikers all stood by their rigs, talking and laughing. He was glad that Eldon had taken a liking to the two guys, especially after they'd helped pull him out of a big mud hole close to Horse Bench Reservoir, which was now full, a rare sight.

Even though Graham and Clara's LTD had become stuck, the road out to the San Rafael Desert and June's Bottom really wasn't too bad now, as most of the mud had already dried up.

This was typical for this country because of the dry humidity and hot sun, and all one usually had to do when they got stuck was just give it some time. The couple could probably go get their car by now if they could get a ride.

The BOB-O's were taking a little break before beginning the tricky descent down to the river. Frosty had been giving the two guys a primer on using your gears instead of your brakes when on steep slopes, while Eldon illustrated Frosty's technical advice with stories of people who had done it wrong.

Bud was glad the mountain bikers had come along, for he not only liked young people, but he also enjoyed seeing Eldon and Frosty get to show off some of their knowledge as desert rats. He knew they would have a good time talking around the campfire that evening, assuming they made it down to the river without problems.

Thinking again of the old Scotsman, Bud wondered if Angus had loved the desert as much as he did. He knew Angus had spent time in this country prospecting for uranium, but that didn't mean anything, other than that he wanted to get rich.

Bud wondered why Angus had decided to make a game of finding his treasure. Sure, he'd said in the article that it was for the spirit of the chase, but what fun would it be if you weren't around to enjoy it?

Of course, Bud thought, Angus had no idea his life would end out here, just as none of us ever know when fate will take us away. It just goes to show that you should never take anything for granted. And what had the old man meant by a witch's tongue?

Now, thinking back again to when he'd driven down to June's

Bottom a year ago, something tickled his memory, something he couldn't quite put his finger on.

He'd stood in this exact same place on the rim as the sun went down, for he had camped up on top and then gone down to the river the next morning, and he recalled seeing something unusual, something to do with the atmosphere or geology.

He remembered it was on the summer solstice, and he'd wished he'd brought his camera to take a photo of it. The canyon country was full of surprises and interesting things, but this had been something really different.

Bud sighed, wishing he could remember. He knew he wasn't getting any younger, and he wondered if he too would someday suffer from something like sundowners. Would Wilma Jean have to tie him to his chair every evening to keep him from wandering out into the backcountry to look at the stars? If so, he hoped she would just let him go, as long as there weren't any big cliffs around.

For some reason, that unsettled feeling was starting to haunt him again, and he had no idea why. He thought he'd pretty much come to grips with Wilma Jean selling the cafe and bowling alley, and he was even excited for her to be getting a plane.

Maybe it was the immensity of the canyons, Bud thought, for they sometimes seemed overwhelmingly big and deep and old and mysterious. There had been times he'd had to go home and seek the comfort of the comfy bungalow, as the countryside had become so inhospitable feeling.

Bud knew it was now time to go, as Eldon was yelling at him and the day was wearing on. They wanted him to lead, since he'd been down more recently than either of them, so he knew he'd better get moving.

As he turned and walked back to the FJ, he wondered again what was right on the tip of his memory, that something he'd seen out here. He just couldn't quite get it.

Oh well, he sighed, it must not have been anything very important or he would remember it. He now needed to concentrate on finding the route below, and somehow everything would work out. It would probably come to him at the least likely time.

Once they got down by the river, he knew all would be well, for he could engage in one of his favorite enterprises—sitting under big cottonwood trees watching the world go by—and it was something that always made him happy.

19

As far as Bud knew, the trail he was leading everyone down was called the June's Bottom Trail and had been built by June Marsing in the 1930s. It was considered remote and challenging in four-wheeling vocabulary, and Bud knew that anything could change, usually for the worse, with one good storm.

But having done the trail before, Bud considered the greatest danger on it to be one's inability to take their eyes off the magnificent panoramic scenery. Trin Alcove Point and Entrada Gap were both visible in the distance, as were portions of Labyrinth Canyon.

The first few miles after one left the River Road were a smooth and flat unassuming two-track, but he remembered a sharp turn that would send you into a gully if you were going too fast. He signaled for the others to slow down just in time.

They made the turn, then navigated a long climb to the top of a hill, where the trail turned into a mixture of slickrock and stretches of sand.

Bud had driven across long stretches of slickrock like this many times, and he knew it was easy to get off trail, but he also knew to stay close to a red Entrada sandstone layer, avoiding the drop-offs and heady cracks that disappeared into the depths of nearby Three Canyon.

He had to stop several times to scope out the trail, but each time, he could see where someone had stacked a rock cairn marking the right direction. Finally, they came to a larger cairn, which marked where one had to turn to the north.

Now the route got trickier, starting the descent into the canyon, dropping down a couple of difficult ledges onto the next level of slickrock.

Bud got out and stopped everyone, making sure Nick and Art had their 4Runner in low gear. He knew Eldon and Frosty had put their hubs in long before, both being seasoned four-wheelers.

"Having fun yet?" he asked.

Art and Nick both shook their heads yes, and Bud wondered if they would feel the same once they got to the bottom, as driving down was much more challenging than riding a bike. Although mountain bikers seemed to be discovering this area more and more, Bud never could understand the attraction in having to push a bike back up the steep route.

They continued downwards, soon reaching the first section where June had obviously spent a considerable amount of time making the trail passable by stacking rocks. Bud once again shook his head at the unbelievable work people did back in the good old days just to survive.

He knew that many of these river bottoms had been the locations of moonshine stills during Prohibition, but he also knew the moonshiners got to them by boat, not by navigating steep canyon walls.

Andy Moore was one of the early pioneers in the area, and he'd staked his claim to June's Bottom, then given permission for June to farm there. June had built a small rock house into the canyon wall, as well as another rock building nearby, probably for food storage. The river bottoms had rich soil where one could successfully grow vegetables and berries, and in addition, June's Bottom had a nice spring for drinking water.

Bud slowly wound his way down the canyon, glad for the recent rain, as it had made the sandy spots firm and easily passable. He thought of June and his family parking their vehicle on top and coming in on ropes before improving the trail.

Bud was once again amazed at how tough the early people into these canyons had been. He'd been down the Flint Trail into what was now Canyonlands National Park, where the Chaffins had once run cattle in an area they called "Under the Ledge."

It amazed him they'd even been able to get stock down in there. He recalled reading about Ned going in alone to take care of the cattle for weeks at a time when he was barely a teen.

As Bud stopped to make sure everyone behind him got across a ledge alright, he thought of the little town of Green River, which had primarily been a railroad town, but still held the descendants of some of the old canyon pioneer stock, one of who was Old Man Green. Bud himself was of such stock, though his ancestors had been further north up at Price, a coal-mining town with a rich history of its own.

They continued slowly until the trail began to narrow, where Bud pulled over and signaled for everyone to stop.

"We're coming to the crux," he said. "I think it would be wise for us to go check it out before proceeding. If it's still wet from the storm, we would probably be wise to turn around."

They all walked down the trail, where it now crossed a slickrock saddle of sorts, then made a sharp turn as it dropped off yet another ledge.

They studied it for awhile, and finally, Eldon said, "Me and Bud and Frosty will be fine, 'cause we all have short wheel bases. But you boys in that 4Runner might want to take a little air out of your left rear tire so you can beat that camber. And if you don't center your vehicle just right, you're gonna tip right over and go off."

"How do we get the air back in?" Art asked, somewhat intimidated.

"I have an air compressor in my FJ," Bud replied. "But it's not 25 years old, so you'll have to ask Eldon if we can use it. Don't forget, this is a BOB-O expedition."

Eldon made a harumph noise, which they took for a yes, then asked, "You boys want me to drive it across for you?"

Art looked nervously at Nick, who said, "No, but thanks for the offer. Art can walk and direct me. I'd like to give it a try."

Bud studied the route a while longer, then said, "You guys can go last and watch us do it. Problem is, you're long enough that your back tire's gonna catch some air. Don't panic, and just ride it out. Watch your spotter and you'll be fine."

What Bud didn't mention was that there was another off-camber spot just ahead, just as tricky as this one, but he didn't want to make them worry any more than they already were.

Bud went first, then Frosty and Eldon, both in their old Willys Jeeps, with no problems. Now they all got out and watched as Art tried to spot Nick across the ledge.

Suddenly, the 4Runner started to take a nosedive, and everyone shouted, "Slow down!" Nick slowed to a crawl and managed to barely clear the edge. Bud thought that Art was about to pass out, his face was so red.

They continued a short distance down until they came to another similar shelf, and Art got out again to spot, this time Nick driving across it just fine.

The rest of the route went down a somewhat heady sidehill over decomposed rock, but it was dry and not slippery, and they were soon going through an old gate and on down to the bottom, driving through thick stands of brush that scratched the sides of their vehicles in what Bud called desert pinstripes.

Once on the bottom, they all talked about the trail, relieved to have made it. Bud knew that going back up would be easier, as one could see out of their vehicles better and knew the trail, but it would still be slow.

After taking a break, they wandered over to look at an old boiler that June had used to pump water from the river to irrigate his vegetables, burning brush for fuel.

Bud took photos of an old axle and assorted wheels and rusted parts, then wandered over to what was left of June's stone house and storage shed, taking more photos. He knew there was an old corral on around the bend, but he decided not to go that far.

Later, in retrospect, Bud was glad he hadn't continued on to the old corral, for unbeknownst to him, someone was camped there, and that particular someone wasn't anyone he especially wanted to talk to.

He eventually made his way back to camp, joining the others, who were listening as Frosty gave a history lesson about John Wesley Powell and his crew floating the river on two separate expeditions in the late 1800s.

As Art and Nick listened with rapt attention, Bud was glad for their company, for he could feel an entirely different level of energy with them there.

His earlier trepidation back at the bungalow seemed to be completely gone, and he knew that coming into the canyons had been the right thing to do.

20

Bud couldn't remember having had more fun. There was just nothing to compare with sitting around a campfire with friends after a fine meal of camp chili and dutch-oven cornbread, shooting the bull, and trying to outdo each other in telling wild tales.

They'd survived the trail down into June's Bottom, and everyone had said he'd done a fine job leading them down to the big sand bar under the trees by the river, where, sadly enough, the tammies were taking over. But it was nice and shady, and the only downside to it all was that he wished the boys were there with him, Hoppie at his feet and little Pierre in his lap.

In addition, Art and Nick had turned out to be a lot of fun and seemed to really be enjoying hearing old stories about the canyon country, of which both Eldon and Frosty had plenty in their repertoire. They would be able to tell their friends their own tales when they got back to Salt Lake, as they'd never done any four-wheeling like this before.

The sun now began to set over the rim, the remnants of the storm clouds catching the fiery rays and turning the sky ruby red. Bud got out his camera, the color of the clouds making him think of the quartz in his pocket, and he felt to make sure it was still there.

Sitting under a big cottonwood in his old canvas camp chair, Eldon remarked, "Indians are killing buffalo."

"How do you know?" Art asked, unfolding his lightweight high-tech chair next to him.

Eldon laughed. "It's an old Western expression for when you see a blood-red sky like this."

"Oh," Art replied. "Cool."

Eldon now wore a colorful tie that looked like something Hank Williams would have liked, with a glittery guitar and giant musical note. The width of the tie made Eldon look even skinnier than he was. He'd put it on, he said, to "dress for dinner."

Not to be outdone, Frosty had put on an equally wide suede leather tie that had the effect of making him look even more stout than he was.

Soon the last rays reflected off the river onto the walls of the canyon, reminding Bud of the treasure poem Howie had read to him, and he asked, "Any of you boys know anything about Mackie's treasure?"

"Whose treasure?" Art asked.

"Angus Mackie, an old Scotsman down in St. George who suppos-edly buried treasure around here somewhere," Frosty answered, somewhat to Bud's surprise.

"Have you read the poem?" Bud asked Frosty.

"I have. In fact, I have a copy of it right here in my pocket."

"Treasure?" asked Art. "You mean as in a box of gold or something like that?"

"Yes, gold in a strongbox. Buried somewhere around these parts," Frosty replied.

"Does the poem actually say it's gold?" Bud asked. "I thought it just said treasure."

"Pretty sure it's gold," Frosty replied. "Here, let me check." He pulled the poem from his pocket.

"Looks like maybe you've been talking to Howie," Bud grinned.

"No, Howie's been talking to me," Frosty replied. "He told me about it and showed me the magazine article. He sent in the money for the poem and let me copy it. Charged me five bucks. Said he was trying to get his money back by sharing it, though that's not exactly how I would define sharing."

"A poem about treasure?" asked Nick, waving the smoke away from his face.

"You're supposed to say 'I like alligators' if you want the smoke to turn," Eldon advised.

"I like alligators," repeated Nick, looking surprised as the smoke turned towards where Bud and Frosty sat.

Bud laughed. "I've never heard that one before."

"You didn't grow up in Louisiana," Eldon replied.

"You didn't either, Eldon," Frosty said. "You grew up in Castle Dale."

"But there's a poem about treasure around here?" Art said, trying to get them back on track.

"Yes, but it won't make any sense to you, I guarantee that," Eldon said. "I personally think it's a big hoax and the old guy was having his last laugh at the world. After all, he's supposed to be in his eighties."

"It's Spanish gold, and I think it's down at Spanish Bottom," Frosty said, ignoring Eldon.

"Is there gold in this country?" Art asked.

"There's placer gold," Bud replied. "But it's so fine and light it's not worth bothering with. It's more over on the Colorado River. A lot of people have spent a lot of money trying to dredge it, pretty much for naught."

"Well," said Frosty, "This is gold coins, not placer gold. Gold coins in a big old metal box."

"Do you mind reading the poem?" asked Nick.

"It's way too long," Eldon replied. "The old guy was a wordy son of a biscuit."

"Nah, let's go through it," Frosty said. "We can do it line by line. These boys might have some fresh ideas. We've pretty much beat the thing to death and got nowhere."

"Read it!" commanded Art.

Bud stood and threw more wood on the fire, the firelight making the glitter on Eldon's tie sparkle and dance.

Now Frosty started reading:

> *You want the riches, treasure trove,*
> *Whose gold will bring you many things,*
> *But stop and ponder on it now,*
> *Before you risk its deadly stings.*

"See," Frosty explained, "Says it's gold. That's just a sort of preamble like storytellers do. He's telling you he's going to tell you something about treasure to get your attention."

> *Begin the search away from rim,*
> *Where light shines up the canyon wall,*
> *From Tumbleweed go 'round the bend,*
> *And you will see where you can't fall.*

"Now it starts getting harder. I'm not sure what he means by 'away from rim.' It seems like he'd say something like 'at the rim,' or 'below the rim.'"

"Maybe he wants you to know it's out there, away, someplace you can see from the rim, way over there, that kind of thing, maybe the opposite side of the river," Art said.

"Makes sense," Frosty replied. "And what about where light shines up the canyon wall, what would that be?"

"Light reflected off the river," Bud said. "And where you can't fall could also be on the water. Howie and I tried to figure it out, and that's what we came up with. But we couldn't figure out the tumbleweed thing."

"Tumbleweeds grow on the rim, so he's just repeating himself," Eldon added as his two bits' worth.

Frosty continued. "OK, here's the next stanza."

> *It's not a place where one walks free,*

But if you search at setting sun,
You'll see the man high in the scree,
His left arm points where search is done.

They all sat in silence, until Nick said, "He's talking about a lot of rocks or rubble—can't walk free—and if you stand in the right place when the sun sets, you'll see someone pointing to it. Man, that makes no sense. Why would someone be standing there pointing to it at sunset?"

"And in the scree," Art said. "More rubble."

Bud felt something stir in his memory, but it didn't quite form a thought.

"Well, you guys are getting this better than I did," Frosty said. "Here's the next one."

You cannot walk, you cannot swim,
You must have wood beneath your feet,
And treasure bright will be too dim,
To guide your light for shore to meet.

"A boat!" Eldon said, excited. "He's talking about a boat! Makes sense with the river thing. You can't walk on the river, it's too big and deep to swim, so you need a boat, something made of wood."

"Holy crackers!" Frosty said. "It has to be a boat. You're a genius!"

"What about the treasure being too dim and all that?" Nick asked.

Art replied, "He's just saying that since it's at setting sun and going to get dark, you need a light of some kind. That's my take on it, anyway."

Frosty continued.

If you are wise and find the way,
Across the hazards as they flow,
Beware of slippery feet of clay,
Walk soft and take in sunset glow.

Now Nick said, "The hazards as they flow—it could mean the river, or maybe it has to be more of the scree type thing. In other words, it's up somewhere higher, where gravity will make rocks and scree or whatever flow down. But I have no idea what the slippery feet of clay could be. Are there some hoodoos around that have clay feet or something?"

"Could be," Frosty said, "But I wouldn't know where."

> *So do it now, and if you fail,*
> *You know your life will be at stake,*
> *For June it is, you've heard the tale,*
> *And summer solstice is the take.*

Now Frosty asked, "Why would it be dangerous?"

Eldon replied, "He's a poet. He's just using that for dramatic effect. Ain't nothin' dangerous around here."

Art added, "Maybe it has some kind of curse associated with it, like a lot of this kind of stuff—you know, like the Hope Diamond."

"Well," Frosty said. "What about the rest of it? What about June? The summer solstice is in June—in fact, it's almost here."

They sat in silence for awhile, then Frosty read the last stanza.

> *The brave will win, the fool will die,*
> *And which you are you soon will know,*
> *For nothing here can be a lie,*
> *And fool's gold treasure lies below.*

Now Eldon chimed in. "See, he says 'fool's gold.' I think it's a big boondoggle, a joke, if it's even really there."

"But he says nothing's a lie," Frosty answered. "How can he say it's not a lie if it's a lie?"

"Any good politician can answer that," Eldon replied, then turned to Art and Nick. "You boys are good at riddle solving. What exactly do you do for a living?"

Nick replied, "I'm a computer programmer, and Art's a linguist.

We both work for a defense contractor. We solve riddles every day as part of our jobs."

"You're spooks?" Eldon asked.

"What's a spook?" Art asked, looking pained, as if he already knew the answer.

"You know, spies. Hopefully you're spying on them and not us."

"Eldon," Frosty said patiently. "We're here to re-create the good old days, not interrogate our guests. It's not good Western etiquette to ask a bunch of questions. Would you be asking Butch Cassidy about his profession if he were here with us?"

"Maybe," Eldon said stubbornly. "And the Cold War was in the good old days, lots of spying going on then, so we're within BOB-O guidelines."

"Well, asking for details when someone tells you they're working for the Defense Department might not be the brightest thing," Frosty said.

"Are you calling me stupid?" Eldon asked testily. "Remember, stupidity is halfway around the world while common sense is still tying its shoes."

"I don't think you understand what that means. That's not a good thing, Eldon," Frosty replied, shaking his head.

Bud grinned, changing the subject. "Any of you ever hear of a witch's tongue?"

Eldon replied, "Is it a kind of plant? Seems like my mom mentioned something like that once, or was that devil's foot or something or other? Other than that, I don't know."

Everyone was now silent, the hot embers dancing as Frosty put more wood on the fire, the gnarled trunks of the old cottonwoods lit with the bright orange of the flames.

Now the talk turned to other worlds and aliens and spacemen, and both Eldon and Frosty had either seen one or knew someone who had, while Art and Nick expressed skepticism. Bud thought of the fellow he'd rescued in his back yard, but said nothing.

Finally, as things got quiet, Bud said, "You know, if tumbleweed's a place of some kind upstream, then 'around the bend' in the poem could refer to the biggest bend in the river in these parts, Trin-Alcove, which is just upriver from us. It says go around the bend. You guys think the June in the poem might just be June Marsing of June's Bottom instead of the month of June?"

No one said a word, pondering the implications of a big chest of Spanish gold somewhere nearby.

Finally, Frosty said, "Bud, I think you might be on to something. Sure is food for thought. I probably won't get a wink of sleep tonight."

Bud stood, saying, "Well, sorry to stir the ants' nest. It was just a thought. But speaking of sleep, I'm going to have to turn in. You guys staying up, or should we put out the fire?"

"We're staying up for awhile," Nick said. "We'll make sure it's out. Good night, and thanks for inviting us. I can't remember when I've had such a good time."

As Bud headed for his tent he could hear Eldon saying, "Let's go over that poem again."

Bud was tired, but in a good way. As he put his longjohns on and slipped into his down bag, he thought for a moment that he could hear something come up to his tent. Whatever it was, it stood there for a minute, and Bud could hear breathing.

He knew there were sometimes deer along these river bottoms, so he figured that's what it was. He recalled reading an oral history by Ned Chaffin where he told about a friend roping a big buck down on Valentine Bottom.

Bud said softly, "I like alligators," and whatever it was left. He then eventually slipped into a fitful sleep, tired and wishing he'd remembered to bring an extra sleeping pad, as the one he had was as old as the good old days and pretty much as hard as a treasure chest of gold coins.

21

Bud leaned against his FJ, partway up the trail to June's Bottom, looking down on the river canyon below. It was early morning, and if he timed it just right, he could get a photo of a sunstar coming across the cliff tops to the east.

He'd been up for what seemed like a long time, drinking coffee he'd made on Frosty's old Coleman stove and waiting for the others to rise.

It had been a long night and he hadn't slept well, and he'd decided he wanted to go home instead of spending another night down on the river with a sore back. He was sure the others would have no trouble getting back out now that they knew the trail.

He'd woken in the wee hours of the night and heard the others still talking around the campfire, so he knew they'd be getting up late. He'd gone back to sleep, but awakened before dawn, quietly taking down his tent and putting everything into the FJ. He'd then sat and waited, drinking coffee and watching the reflective eyes of a hoot owl in the trees above that was probably looking for field mice.

After having a bowl of cereal with some canned milk, he then busied himself gathering wood for the BOB-O's fire that night, as he knew they would probably spend the day there looking for Mackie's treasure.

He wondered if Art and Nick would give Eldon and Frosty instruction on riding fat-tired bikes, maybe even drinking Fat Tire Ale while doing so.

Eldon finally was up and around, and Bud handed him a cup of coffee, telling him he was going on home instead of staying another day. Eldon understood, as he hadn't slept so well himself, as he had a hole in his tent where the mosquitoes were getting through.

Soon Frosty was also up, and Bud said his goodbyes and started up the hill, leaving his tent for Eldon, not waiting for Art and Nick to get up.

It had taken awhile to climb partway out of the canyon in the dim light, but now that Bud had passed the crux, he'd decided to take a break and watch the sunrise and get some photos.

He'd taken some time to frame a shot to include an old dead juniper tree, and as the sun broke over the rim, he took a half-dozen photos, then studied his camera's LED.

He was pleased to see he had several good sunstar photos, and by the time he'd put his camera back into the FJ, the sun had risen enough to clear the rim and shine on something down in the bottom of the canyon.

Bud got out his binoculars, and to his surprise, he saw a tan two-door Jeep parked near the old corral, back where it wouldn't be visible from their camp below. As Bud watched, he saw someone appear to take down a tent and put it in the Jeep, then get in and slowly start making their way along the river bottom.

How in hellsbells had the Jeep gotten in there without them hearing or seeing it? The only explanation was that it had been there before they arrived. He watched as it drove right by their camp, stopped for a moment as if talking to Frosty and Eldon, then headed on up, following the trail.

Now Bud recalled someone standing by his tent the previous night, and he now knew it hadn't been a deer or animal, but was instead Ryder Gates. He must've figured out that the treasure was somewhere around June's Bottom and gone down there looking for it, or maybe he'd overheard them in the store and beat them out there, intending to spy on them.

Either way, Bud found it irritating that Ryder had probably been eavesdropping on their conversation the previous night. After all, hadn't he admitted to being a treasure hunter? What irritated Bud the most was his skulking around, as they would've been more than happy to share their dinner and conversation with him if he'd just been upfront about it all. And now he appeared to be following him —or was he just being paranoid?

In any case, Bud had no intention of meeting up with the guy, as he'd struck him as being a bit rough around the edges, and knowing he'd probably been standing by his tent the night before didn't set well with him. Maybe he had wanted to talk to him and changed his mind when Bud mentioned alligators.

He was soon back in the FJ and making good time up the trail, pushing it a little harder than he preferred, but determined that he would leave Ryder in the dust.

Finally on top, he briefly wondered again what he'd seen on his last trip that had slipped his mind, but he didn't stop to think about it. He was now headed back to where the June's Bottom spur road met the River Road, glad he was heading west so the sun wasn't in his eyes.

He could see the head of Three Canyon to his right, the road going out and around it, as the canyon dropped straight off, eventually feeding into the Green. Bud had heard that an old and very rugged cattle trail accessed the mouth of the canyon by traversing the talus above the river, but he'd never seen it.

Once back at the intersection with the main road, Bud knew he had about 30 miles of fairly smooth driving back to Green River, though it typically took an hour or more. He relaxed, not seeing any sign of Ryder in his rear-view mirror.

He would spend some time taking photos, then surprise Wilma Jean by coming home early, and maybe even go hang out at the airport with her for awhile, checking out the new plane. He wondered if they'd managed to put the wings back on it yet.

Crossing the bridge over the San Rafael River, he noted the river seemed to be running a little higher than usual, probably from the big rain. He thought of stories he'd read about the old-time cowboys having to ride bog, as they called it, searching for cattle stuck in the quicksand along the small river, then trying to pull them out with a rope.

Those were the good old days that Eldon missed, Bud thought wryly. Interestingly enough, as the tamarisk had moved into the country, displacing the willows and native riparian vegetation, the quicksand had mostly disappeared, for tammies were water sinks and sucked everything dry, their roots going down 30 feet or more.

Bud soon came to the intersection with the road to the old Chaffin Ranch with its old corrals and homestead at the confluence of the San Rafael and Green. Without even thinking about it, he made a quick right-hand turn, and was soon bouncing down the rough two-track.

He was glad for the previous rain, as it meant there wouldn't be much of a rooster tail of dust following him, and hopefully Ryder wouldn't know he'd turned off there. He wanted some time alone to maybe get in some photography, and if Ryder thought he would follow Bud to treasure or anything of significance, he was in for a big surprise.

Knowing there was a small geyser on the road to the ranch, Bud decided to stop there and try his hand at photographing it. He could hang out there all day, enjoying the quiet, waiting for it to erupt, though he knew it was small and wouldn't do much. Maybe he could get some good ground shots that would make it look bigger.

He finally reached the geyser, where, to his surprise, he saw a pickup with the words, "Utah Geological Society," on its side.

Pulling over, Bud was disappointed to see a young man and woman over by the geyser, looking down into its bubbling pots. He was hoping for some solitude, as he was a bit self-conscious about his photography, and people always wanted to see what he was doing.

Just then, the geyser started to blow, and Bud could see they were both soaked as they jumped back, laughing.

Maybe it wouldn't be so bad after all, he thought, getting out of the FJ. If they were geologists, maybe he could learn something about geysers, and maybe they could tell him more about the rock in his pocket.

22

"Isn't this a fun little geyser?" the woman asked Bud. "It's so pretty, too. No wonder it's called Champagne Geyser. Look at the water, it looks just like the bubbly."

The geyser was now in full eruption, reaching maybe all of six feet, and Bud thought that it did seem to bubble like champagne. It was surrounded by wide terraces of beautiful deep orange and purple travertine.

"I thought it was called Chaffin Geyser," he replied.

"It is," said the man. "It's actually called both. Chaffin is the more historic name, though."

"I like Champagne better," said the woman. Both she and her co-worker were lean and fit with dark hair, and Bud thought they could be brother and sister.

"I'm Bud Shumway," he offered. "I live in Green River."

"Lucky you," replied the woman. "We have to come down from Salt Lake to see stuff that's just out your back door. I'm May and this is my cousin Brandon. Our grandparents were both geologists and we're following the family tradition. But you're out early."

"I camped down by the river last night," Bud replied. "Thought I'd come by and see the geyser. I've read a little about it—it was drilled by the Chaffins as a water source for their nearby ranch. They really had to hardscrabble it to get the drill and all, and when they hit water they were really excited, but when they tasted it and found out it was hard, they were beyond disappointed."

"That would be very disappointing. If we had any idea how hard things were for the early people around here..." Brandon's voice trailed off.

Bud asked, "Are you guys studying the geology around here?"

"We are," Brandon replied. "We're both working on our PhDs at the University of Utah. We're working with the geological service. We'll be out here off and on all summer."

"Just how many geysers are around here, anyway?" Bud asked. "I know of Crystal Geyser and the Airport Geyser and this one, but are there a lot of others?"

"Airport Geyser?" May asked. "Where's that?"

"I bet it's out by the airport," Brandon grinned. "But that's a new one on us."

"It's just across the road from the airport gate," Bud replied. "There's a small stand of tammies there."

"Tammies?" asked May.

"Tamarisk," Brandon answered. "That stuff's sure invasive, isn't it? But it has led us to a couple of geysers. But let's see, so far, we have Crystal Geyser, Chaffin/Champagne Geyser, Big and Little Bubblies..."

"Where are those?" Bud asked.

Brandon replied, "They're over on the other side of the river. There are a few over there, kind of by Ten Mile Canyon. So far, if we count the one you just told us about, we have ten. That doesn't include the one up by Woodside, as it's too far away for our study."

"What causes them?" Bud asked.

"Well, that's part of what we're trying to figure out," May said. "These are all cold water, which is a very rare thing in the world of geysers. Most of them were created in the 1930s and 40s by drilling exploration wells, looking for oil. Crystal Geyser is the biggest, and it was drilled in 1937. We do know that the wells hit a layer of carbon dioxide being sequestered in the sandstone, which is probably migrating upwards from a layer of limestone. The difference in pressure between the carbon dioxide and the surface atmosphere eventually results in an eruption."

"Interesting," Bud said, watching as the small geyser erupted itself out, going back to just a small bubbling pool. "But what exactly do you do out here to study them?"

Brandon said, "We take water samples and do probes and examine the formations in the vicinity, as well as time the eruptions. Once we collect our data, we'll go back and put it all together—we'll make a grid of geysers and where they're located and their elevations and all that and see how they interconnect. That will help us see what's beneath, where the carbon dioxide is and how deep. Carbon dioxide sequestering is a hot topic right now, with all the stuff going into the atmosphere. All this Navajo Sandstone Formation is perfect as a holding tank. It's dense and holds stuff, that's why they thought it might have oil."

"That's a bit of a simplification," May smiled. "Sandstones are coarser grained and have low to high permeabilities, and since CO_2 is buoyant in water, it rises to the top of the formation, so you need a shale or mudstone as a seal above the sandstone so the gas can't pass through. But we met a guy out here from Great Britain studying it. His name was Kit, and he said the geology here was analogous to North Sea storage sites for industrial CO_2. People are starting to come from all over to study it here, as it's relatively easy to get to."

"And interesting country," Brandon added.

"Agreed," Bud replied, thinking of the rock in his pocket. He pulled out the quartz, and handed it to May.

"Do you guys have any idea what this might be?"

She held the rock up to the sun, rolled it around in her hands, then handed it to Brandon. He did the same, tried to bite into it, then handed it back to Bud.

"Is it rose quartz?" Bud asked.

"Where did it come from?" Brandon asked.

"I found it out here," Bud replied. "Actually, over by Airport Geyser. That's a travertine coating, I think."

"I don't think there's any way that's a native rock," May replied. "Someone brought it out here. It's not quartz."

"I'm not sure what it is, but it's very hard, almost like a diamond, but the color's all wrong," Brandon said. "And a diamond that big would probably be behind a glass wall with armed guards like at London Tower. You say you found it? It's odd that it's faceted, isn't it?"

"I think so, too," Bud said, putting the rock back into his pocket. "Probably a necklace or something someone lost. I sure wish I could figure out what it is."

"It's not quartz," May repeated. "It could be selenite or something like that, but it feels too hard. It would be hard to facet selenite or even quartz."

Bud replied, "Well, I'm going on down to the old Chaffin Ranch to take some photos. Good luck on your geyser work. Do you think you'll be finding any more?"

May replied, "We're sure there are more out here, if we could just find them. We keep looking and looking, but usually what we think are geysers turn out to just be shadows in the rocks. This desert can be very elusive."

"Well, I'm sure we'll meet again. Stop in at the Melon Rind Cafe when you're in town. My wife owns it," Bud replied, then added, "At least for now. She may be selling it."

He got into his FJ as they waved goodbye, then drove on down the old road. The Chaffin Ranch was near the Green River, and as he dropped down, he could see the extensive irrigated alfalfa fields across the river at Ruby Ranch.

Once at the old Chaffin homestead, he poked around in the ruins, taking a photo of the remnants of an old rusted-out wheelbarrow leaning against the weathered corral posts. Nobody else was around, which was how he liked it, now sure that Ryder hadn't followed him.

Finally, after taking lots of photos, he leaned back against his FJ, eating a peanut butter and jam sandwich and drinking a warm can of root beer. He was finally really enjoying himself, though he was once again missing the dogs, knowing they would've really liked being out there with him.

He again wondered what the rock in his pocket was, thinking of how May and Brandon had seemed as perplexed as he was. He was a little envious of them, being so young and yet knowing what they wanted to do with their lives, studying geysers and geology and all that. He next recalled what May had said about how potential geysers often turn out to just be shadows in the rocks.

It now hit Bud like a ton of bricks as he remembered what it was that he'd seen that day up on the rim above June's Bottom, and it indeed was something unusual.

He hadn't realized, as he'd stood there that day, gazing off into the distance, that what he saw could someday be important. He now knew it was what he needed to solve the riddle of Mackie's treasure, as well as maybe figure out what the mysterious tumbleweed was. It could possibly even help him solve what had happened to Angus.

And he also knew that time was of the essence.

23

Bud pulled over by the airport hanger, disappointed to see that Wilma Jean's Lincoln wasn't in front. He knew she would be there if at all possible, so he figured she was busy at the cafe.

Now that he was here, there was no reason to not go on inside and see the new plane. He could tell that Sammy, the airport manager, was there from the old pickup parked nearby. Sammy did mechanical work when a plane needed it, as well as air traffic control, which is what he called turning on the airport lights at night.

"Hey, Bud!" Sammy greeted him warmly. "You just missed your wife. She said she had to go to the bowling alley. I guess somebody forgot to show up or something."

"Where's the plane?" Bud asked.

"Come on inside," Sammy replied, opening the side door into the hanger.

"Ain't it a beaut?" Sammy asked, nodding towards a small plane with bright yellow paint and one wing missing. It had black lightning bolts painted down both sides. "That old Vern, man, you have to hand it to him. What a horse trader."

"How so?" Bud asked, walking around the plane and sizing it up. "This isn't a very big plane, is it?"

Sammy answered, "Only one pilot and one passenger, which makes it better if you crash it, not as many injured. You're looking at one of, if not *the*, best outback planes ever made by a human being. This little Piper Cub will take you where few people can go, land you safely, and get you back out again. It's legendary."

"How did Vern get it?"

"He told me that some guy landed it out at the Hidden Splendor airstrip and couldn't get it going again. He was real lucky that Vern just happened to be flying a pilot friend in to show him the strip and found the guy stranded there."

Sammy wiped his hands on his pants, then continued, "Vern flew the guy back to Hanksville, where he got his wife to agree to trade her big Buick for the plane. He and his friend went back and put some gas in it, and it took right off. Vern thought he was a real smart cookie, but when he got it to Hanksville, it wouldn't start again. I went down and took a look at it, but couldn't find what's wrong, so Vern decided to bring it up here and have me do a complete restoration. I'm gonna be busy for awhile, I guess, and his bargain plane could end up costing him a fortune."

"What do you think the plane's worth?" Bud asked.

"Like it is? About what the old Buick was worth. Restored? I dunno, maybe considerably more. Hard to say, as they didn't make a lot of this model, but it is an old plane. But I doubt if it has much wrong with it, as it was a pretty bombproof model."

"I know Wilma Jean's hoping to buy it from Vern," Bud said. "But I'm wondering where we'll get the money."

Sammy offered Bud a stick of licorice gum. "She told me she thinks she has a buyer for the cafe," Sammy said.

"That was fast," Bud remarked, surprised. "Way too fast. I haven't even got used to the idea of selling it yet, Sammy. Where am I going to sit around drinking coffee when I need to get away from everything?"

"What happened to the Chow Down?" Sammy asked. "Didn't you hang around there a lot when you were sheriff, eating donuts?"

Bud laughed. "I did. But I had to give it up, as my wife got upset."

"She wanted you to eat at the Melon Rind? I thought they didn't serve donuts."

"No, she wanted me to pretty much not eat at all." Bud patted his stomach. "I'm on a diet, but I can't seem to stick with it."

"I've been on a diet my whole life," Sammy replied, picking up a wrench. "A try-it diet. I try everything that looks good."

Bud laughed. "Say, do you ever talk to Tim Wells? I sure enjoyed flying over the slickrock around Radium with him. I'll never forget that."

Sammy said, "Last I heard, he was still flying tourists all over the place. I've seen what I thought was his plane a few times recently, probably flying treasure hunters around. What a boondoggle that is. Whoever got that one started should be shot, except I guess it is stirring up some business around these parts."

Sammy paused to turn on a bright light above the plane, then continued. "No offense to anyone, Bud, but in my opinion, most pilots have rocks in their heads, and that Wells family has more than usual. I'd much rather fix these darn things than fly them. But say, you mind helping me lift this wing into place? I can't lift it and tighten it on at the same time."

Bud helped Sammy with the wing, surprised by how light it was.

"How much does this whole plane weigh?" he asked.

Sammy replied, "Empty, 765 pounds. You can lift off in this thing at 50 miles per hour. This little J-3 may be old, but it's still the finest backcountry plane on the road. And I mean that literally—you can land these anywhere, including on the road if you have to. Your wife can start flying this before she gets her full license, as it qualifies as a light sport aircraft and all you need is the sport license."

Bud wasn't sure if that would be a good thing or not, so he just nodded.

Sammy continued, "The stall speed is 38 m.p.h., but all you have to do if you stall it is pull back the throttle and it will recover itself. But notice it's a tail dragger—see that little wheel back there is all you've got—which means she'll have to learn a bit different landing technique than in Vern's 150. But this plane will go anywhere. It's the best bush plane ever made, though the Top Cub's pretty special, too, but it's only a mere quarter million."

Bud nodded appreciatively, thinking again about flying into scenic spots and taking photos. Finally, he said, "I guess I need to get going. I'm tired. I went down to June's Bottom last night with the BOB-O's and forgot my good sleeping pad."

"June's Bottom?" Sammy asked. "I haven't been down there for years. My granddad knew June Marsing. I remember him telling me that he asked him once where he got the name of June, and he told him it was short for Junior."

"That's interesting," Bud said. "I've always thought it was an unusual name for a guy. Say, Sammy, where exactly is Vern? Wilma Jean said he was going to help you put the plane back together."

"He was here for awhile," Sammy answered. "But he got a last-minute job. Some kid came in and wanted him to fly him up the river. He looked pretty rough, didn't even have matching shoes. Vern made him pay in advance."

"Where did he take him?"

"The kid said he had a plane he wanted to go pick up. He must be related to the Wells family, 'cause if he has a license, he started out pretty young."

"Where was the plane?"

"The strip at Sand Wash," Sammy replied. "He said he'd rafted down the river and needed to go back for it. Anyway, I gotta get busy, Bud. Nice talking to you."

With that, he opened the cowling and stuck his head under it.

"See you around, Sammy," Bud said. "Thanks for the gum."

24

"No, it wasn't an offer to buy the cafe," Wilma Jean told Bud, "That's not what I told Sammy at all. This is why this little town always has all these rumors making the rounds."

She was stretched out on the couch in her pink floral pajamas and big white fluffy faux-fur slippers, Hoppie sleeping at her feet. Bud sat in his big recliner opposite them in his Scooby Doo PJs and leather slippers, which Pierre was busy chewing on.

"He's going to ruin those, hon," Wilma Jean said, and Bud shook his foot until the little dog released his grip. Pierre growled, jumped back onto his slipper like he was killing a mouse, and went right back to chewing away.

"I can always get another pair," Bud said. "He's having too much fun."

"Why don't you give him the ones he already chewed holes in instead of letting him ruin your new ones?" she asked.

"He won't chew on them unless I'm wearing them," Bud replied. "I think it has something to do with live prey versus dead prey. He can tell the difference. But why would Sammy say you had an offer on the cafe when you don't?"

"He just wants it to be true 'cause he knows I want to sell it," she replied. "I didn't have an offer to buy it, but I did have an offer to lease part of it. There's a big difference."

"Lease part of it?" Bud asked as he again shook Pierre free. "How do you lease part of a cafe? Are they wanting to use the kitchen for baking or something?"

"I wish they would lease the bowling alley," Wilma Jean replied, ignoring his question. "You know, Bud, I've been thinking about this a lot. I think I'm going to take the cafe off the market until the bowling alley sells. I'd rather sell it first. I like the cafe a lot better. It's a more sociable place and not as noisy. All those clanking pins get to me."

She now sat up, saying, "I forgot. Your gift arrived today."

"My gift?"

"Well, surely it's a gift and not for you."

Bud knew instantly that she was talking about the ice-cream maker.

"Well," he fumbled for a moment, then recovered. "You're right. It's for Howie and Maureen. She said I should get one, so I figured she must want one herself—you know how people will tell you to get yourself something they wish they had. It's a housewarming gift."

"And you do intend to test it out before giving it to them, right?" she asked knowingly.

Bud sighed. "I was thinking it might be a good idea. Put those frozen strawberries to use before they get freezer burned."

"Right," she agreed. "Probably need to use them all up before long, as well as the other fruit in there. Hon, I think that's a great idea. But instead of giving it away, we'll keep it, and we can advertise home-made ice cream at the cafe. You can help me make several batches each day before you go down to the farm."

Bud groaned. "It's hand cranked. It'll take forever to make enough for the cafe. Let's just give it to Howie and Maureen."

Wilma Jean laughed as she went into the kitchen, returning with two dishes of homemade ice cream, complete with strawberries.

"I already tried it out," she informed Bud. "But this isn't going to be a regular thing. Neither of us needs to start eating ice cream all the time."

Bud took the dish, surprised that his wife hadn't noticed that he already ate ice cream all the time—unless the big dollops he put into his coffee didn't count.

"Delicious," Bud said appreciatively. "But what part of the cafe did you lease out? Is someone wanting to use the big fridge in the back or something?"

"No," she replied. "This guy came in and wanted to be able to do some kind of survey, so I told him he could use one of the booths. I know that sounds strange, but he's going to give out stuff to people who will take the survey, kind of like a bank when you open a new account. It won't take but a few minutes for each person and will be fairly unobtrusive, so he says."

"What kind of survey is it?"

"He said it was basically just asking people questions to try and get an idea of how they viewed the world," Wilma Jean replied.

"How they viewed the world? Like in religion or something?" Bud asked.

"No, it's not like that," she answered. "He said he's a psychologist and he's working for a company that's trying to assess how people in small towns differ in their viewpoints from those in the city. Since the Melon Rind is where the locals eat, he thought it would be a good place to get them to take his survey."

Bud finished the ice cream, Pierre continuing to chew on his slipper, and it now felt like his little teeth were about to break through to his bare foot.

He replied, "Is he from some marketing company trying to figure out how you think so they can manipulate you into buying more junk?"

"Just hold your horses, Mr. Shumway. I already thought of all that and asked him. I wouldn't lease out a booth to just anybody, you know that. He said he's not doing any kind of marketing, it's more of a psychological study. He said it's for a government agency, and I didn't want to get too nosy, but I figure it's for something like the Department of Health."

"Well," Bud replied. "I guess it *is* voluntary. What kind of stuff is he offering for taking his survey?"

"I'm not sure," Wilma Jean replied. "He's starting tomorrow, so you can go down and take it and see. He said it's only going to be for a few days."

Bud now took his slipper off and lightly smacked Pierre on the rear with it, who yelped and ran to Wilma Jean, hiding under her feet, giving Bud a dark look of betrayal.

Bud laughed, calling the little dog, who came over and rolled onto his back at Bud's feet.

"You didn't expect the prey to fight back, did you?" Bud asked, rubbing Pierre's tummy. He then went into the kitchen, returning with biscuits for the dogs.

"You want more ice cream, hon?" He asked his wife just as the door bell rang.

"Who could that be at this time of night?" Wilma Jean asked, and Bud thought he recognized the voice as she opened the door.

"I'm sorry to bother you, Mrs. Shumway, but your husband said I could stay in your trailer. I'll only be a couple of nights. I need a place while I try to find my grandfather."

Bud groaned to himself as Wilma Jean opened the door and invited Duncan to come inside.

25

Bud lay in bed beside his wife, Hoppie at their feet and Pierre down under the covers. He was thinking about how it must have felt for Howie as a rookie sheriff to always need to ask him for advice.

Howie hadn't been a deputy for very long when Bud had announced he was quitting, so everything that came down the pike had been new to him, and Howie's overactive imagination had often made things even worse than they actually were, resulting in some interesting adventures.

At one time, Maureen had even made Howie wear a bracelet with the initials, "WWBD?," which stood for "What Would Bud Do?" encouraging Howie to pretend like he was Bud and act accordingly instead of always calling for advice. The bracelet had slowed things down some for Bud, but Howie still called regularly.

But now it was Bud's turn. It was too late to call Howie, but he desperately wished he could ask him how to deal with Duncan, who was probably now sleeping like a baby in their Airstream trailer, a gift from Wilma Jean's wealthy cousin Juno over in Colorado.

It wasn't actually Duncan himself that presented the problem, but it was more the fact that Duncan's grandfather was deceased, and Duncan had announced that he was going to spend the rest of his days looking for the old guy until he found him. He'd had Vern fly him to Sand Wash so he could get his plane, which had apparently been a gift from his grandfather, and he intended to fly the canyons looking for the old guy. It still wasn't clear to Bud why Duncan had left the plane there and floated down the river.

Bud felt he needed to tell Duncan his grandfather was dead, but he also knew that Howie wanted to talk to him before they eliminated him as a murder suspect. But why would Duncan be trying to find Angus if he'd been the one to kill him? Bud knew that some people were very clever, and Duncan could be using it as a ruse to throw them off track.

"Hon," Wilma Jean now said, "One of us needs to go sleep on the couch."

Bud knew that "one of us" would be him, so he got up, grabbed a blanket and pillow, and headed for the couch, where he tossed and turned even more.

Finally, he got up and went into the kitchen, grabbing a bite of strawberry ice cream, then stood at the back door, where he thought he could see light coming from the Airstream down by the barn.

Duncan must still be awake, Bud thought. Maybe he should just go out and talk to him, tell him about Angus, and let the chips fall where they may. After all, what could Howie ask that would either exonerate Duncan or determine his guilt? Bud had been involved in a number of mysterious cases, way more than Howie had, and he had no idea what he himself would ask.

There would be no point in asking Duncan where he'd been, for Bud knew he could neither prove nor disprove Duncan's whereabouts at the time the old guy had been killed.

Maybe Duncan could come up with an alibi, but if he was still wandering around the desert, looking for treasure, Bud doubted he would have been around anyone. But not having an alibi didn't make him a murderer.

Now Bud thought about the copy of the map he'd made and put into his pocket with the rock. He didn't recall seeing it since he'd washed the shirt, accidentally leaving the rock in it.

He groaned. He'd undoubtedly let it go through the wash with the rock, and it had probably been shredded and gone on down the drain. Shoots, Bud thought, How could he have been so careless?

He now got up and wandered into the laundry room and dug around in the washing machine, then the dryer, looking through the lint holder and even the trash can, but there was no sign of it.

Bud went back into the living room and sat down, disappointed in himself. Duncan had made such a big deal of the map, and now he'd forgotten all about it, letting his copy just go on down the drain into wherever such stuff ended up, probably the septic tank under the big alfalfa field.

It then dawned on him that the key holder might still be on the FJ, and if so, it would have the original map inside.

Bud quietly tiptoed back into the bedroom, grabbing his Herman Survivor boots, then went into the living room and pulled them on. Grabbing a flashlight, he carefully slipped out the kitchen door and was soon under his FJ, feeling inside the frame for the key holder. It took awhile to find it, as Duncan had moved it to a different spot, but Bud soon had it in hand.

He went back inside and sat back down on the couch, turning on the nearby reading lamp, then opened the key holder and took out the map.

It was as cryptic as ever, with the word "Tumbleweed" and the directional lines going out to various letters. He sat there as if in a trance, knowing he should be able to figure it all out, but it just didn't make any more sense than before, and why had he thought it would?

He knew it had to be something that Angus had come up with, and if the treasure poem was any indication of how the old Scotsman's mind worked, why would this be any clearer?

Finally, Bud collapsed into his recliner, pushing it as far back as it would go, tucking the blanket around him. It wasn't long until his lack of sleep at June's Bottom caught up with him, and he was out like a baby, snoring softly.

26

Someone tapped lightly on the back door, and Bud jerked awake. It was still dark outside, and he didn't want whoever it was to wake Wilma Jean and the dogs, so he quickly jumped to his feet, quietly turning on the kitchen light. He could see that the dog with the wagging tail and clock on its tummy read 3 a.m.

He suspected it was probably Duncan at the door, but why in the world would he be waking him at this hour of the night? He hoped it wasn't an emergency of some kind.

Looking out the back porch window into the darkness, Bud couldn't make out anything but a big splotch of white, and he wondered why the moon would be full this time of month, lighting things up.

He turned on the porch light and nearly fell backwards. It was a spaceman! Its big white helmet bobbed around and he could now see that it was trying to signal him to open the door.

Bud wasn't sure that would be a prudent action, so he stood there for a moment, then decided it must be Lieutenant Esker. Was he stuck in his helmet again? And what was he doing out at this time of night?

Bud carefully opened the door far enough that he could now see the spaceman wasn't wearing the rest of his suit, but rather had on a green plaid cowboy-style shirt with khaki pants and black boots. A holster and gun hung off its side, and Bud could almost make out what it was saying.

He stepped outside, closing the kitchen door behind him so as to not wake Wilma Jean, the thing was making so much noise. He tried as he could to make out what it was saying, but it was just gibberish. Maybe it wanted a dish of homemade strawberry ice cream, it was so skinny.

Finally, Bud realized it had to be Howie!

He put his arms around the big helmet, unscrewing it, thinking of how he was becoming a pro at spacesuit extrication, wondering if there might be a future in it someday.

"Man, I thought I was gonna die in there," Howie said, sweat running down his face. "I didn't know what to do, so I came out here. I'm lucky you knew how to get that thing off, Sheriff. I was about to expire from claustrophobia."

"I've done it a time, well, or two, now," Bud grinned. "But Howie, how did you come to have a spacesuit helmet on in the first place?"

"I don't know, Bud. I just woke up and there it was. Maureen was still asleep, and I didn't want to worry her, so I knew I had to come get your help. I knew it has something to do with those spacemen we saw the other night, and now I'm really worried that it's some kind of test to see how well I do in a suit so they can make me go mine minerals on other planets."

Bud laughed, as it all seemed really strange. He knew Howie was playing some kind of joke on him, even though he seemed sincere.

"Maybe you've been sleepwalking. But why 3 a.m., Howie? Isn't there a better time for all this?" Bud asked.

"I would agree, Bud. They're getting out of control."

Bud replied, "Howie, are you and Maureen having some kind of problems? Is there something you want to talk to me about? Where did you get this thing, anyway, down at the high-school drama club?"

"I told you, Bud, but I don't blame you for not believing me."

"It's OK, Howie. I'm actually glad you're here. I've been having trouble sleeping, and I was wishing I could talk to you."

"About what?" Howie asked.

"That guy Duncan," Bud replied.

"Didn't you say someone named Duncan was Angus Mackie's next of kin some time back?" Howie asked.

"Yes, he's Angus Mackie's grandson. He's out in the Airstream. He has a plane, and he says he's not leaving until he finds his grandfather. I know I need to tell him Angus is dead, Howie, but how do I do that and not jeopardize the case?"

Howie shook his head. "Do you think he killed his grandfather?"

Bud felt confused. "I guess it's possible, though I'm not so sure. But how do I tell him so he's not out looking for Angus, and yet not compromise our investigation?"

"Don't be silly, Sheriff," Howie replied. "You know Duncan didn't do it. Angus told us who did it."

"He did?" Bud was mystified.

"Don't you remember? He said it was a witch's tongue." Howie now seemed somewhat irritated. "A witch's tongue killed Angus, Bud, remember?"

"I don't even know what that is, Howie," Bud replied.

"I don't either, Sheriff."

"Could Duncan be a witch?" Bud asked, though he knew it didn't make any sense.

"No," Howie replied. "Witches are always female. If it had been a male, he would've said a warlock's tongue."

"But did he say it had killed him? If I recall, he just cussed it."

Howie replied, "He implied it pretty strongly."

Bud sighed. This was going nowhere. Why Howie was out here in the first place was a mystery to him, and his helmet joke really wasn't very funny.

Finally, Bud said, "Well, since you're here, come inside and take a look at this map and tell me what you think. But don't wake Wilma Jean."

They went inside, Howie carrying the helmet, and Bud took

Duncan's map from the key holder and spread it out on the kitchen table. "Want some strawberry ice cream?" he asked.

"No thanks," Howie said. "I just had some space food sticks before coming out here."

"Don't you mean fish sticks?"

"No, don't you remember space food sticks? They were created for the early astronauts. We used to buy them for camping. Long rubbery sticks that tasted like caramel."

Bud studied Howie for a moment, wondering if he hadn't maybe gotten into some of Old Man Green's hard cider. It wouldn't be the first time, though Howie had claimed the other time was an accident.

Now Howie held the map up, saying, "Bud, this is pretty simple. See, how it all goes out from Tumbleweed? See all these letters—C, TM, PTM, T, TS, BB, LB, SS, C/C, A—it's pretty obvious to me. Don't you see it?"

"Not really," Bud said, frowning.

"OK, think about it. For example, what could C/C be?"

"I don't know."

"OK, how about BB and LB and C and A? You know what those are, don't you? Think back. It's just so obvious." Howie shook his head.

"No idea." Bud was getting depressed.

"OK," Howie said. "Let me give you a hint. Remember when you were talking to the two students doing the geyser research?"

Bud nodded his head yes, though he couldn't recall telling Howie about it.

"Remember what they called the geyser there?"

"Champagne?"

"Yes, but it had another name," Howie said.

"Chaffin," Bud replied.

"Yes, Chaffin, or Champagne/Chaffin. You know, C/C." Howie looked at Bud, then shook his head as if he was dealing with a stubborn child. He then added, "I gotta go. If Maureen wakes up and sees I'm gone, she'll be calling the sheriff, which would be me, I guess. It sometimes gets too confusing, Bud, just like your little map here. And just for the record, BB and LB are Big Bubbly and Little Bubbly, A is for Airport, and the C is Crystal. These letters are all abbreviations for geysers. I would've thought that you would've figured that out by now."

With that, Howie slipped out the door, taking the helmet with him.

Bud suddenly woke, part of his blanket tangled around his head like a space helmet.

It took him awhile to realize he'd been dreaming, it had seemed so real. But he was wide awake with a startle when he realized that his subconscious had finally figured out the map.

Since Bud wouldn't pay attention, it had conjured up a strange dream to make him listen. It wasn't the first time Bud had gone through this.

He tapped his fingers on the side table next to the recliner, thinking, then got up to make coffee. The dog clock read 6 a.m.

Bud now knew what the old Scot had been trying to tell him and Howie as he was dying, and now that he knew what the message was, he felt obligated to pass it on to Mackie's grandson, just as the old man had asked him to.

He would have to tell Duncan that his grandfather was dead and that he'd left a message for him—the message being that Tumbleweed is a geyser, whatever significance that might have.

27

Bud crawled out from under the big John Deere 6140, wiping the grease from his hands onto his blue and white striped coveralls. Even though it had only been a couple of days, it seemed like a long time since he'd been on the farm, and he was feeling a little guilty, even though his part-time assistant, Kale, had been keeping an eye on things. There wasn't a whole lot he could do until the fields dried up anyway, though there was always the never-ending job of equipment maintenance.

Bud had been there since shortly after dawn when he'd gone out to the Airstream and, finding Duncan was still asleep, had decided to go to work instead of waking him to tell him his grandfather was dead. He had instead left him a note saying that he had a message for him from Angus Mackie, that Tumbleweed is a geyser.

He wondered if that wasn't a somewhat round about way to deal with the problem, but it had worked, so far, at least. He'd done what the old man had asked him to, and now it was out of his hands.

He was still tired from what now amounted to several nights of sketchy sleep, and he really just wished he could go sit in the shade and take a nap.

Taking a long drink of cool water from his red water jug, he leaned back against the work bench for a moment, still somewhat disoriented from the weird dream he'd had the previous night about Howie.

He'd tried all morning while working on the tractor to make a mental list of all the known geysers in the area, recalling that May had said they knew of at least 10, if you counted Airport Geyser.

He hadn't really paid much attention to her at the time, not realizing its importance, but he now wished he could go back out and get them to list all the geysers for him, as there were indeed 10 on Duncan's map, but he had no idea where the geologist pair might be by now.

He'd been able to identify one more—Ten Mile, or TM—and he had a hunch the names would match perfectly with the initials on the map if he could just figure them out.

But what good would knowing the names of all the geysers do? And why had Tumbleweed been the center of it all? And where exactly was Tumbleweed?

Even though he felt he'd figured out the symbols on the map, it still made no sense. And what about the little poem at the bottom about a stubborn Scot flying away?

Now Bud studied the calendar above his workbench. It was a photo of a colorful sundog that Bud had seen once out by Drunkard's Wash near Price.

He'd been out rockhounding with his Uncle Joe, his dad's brother up there, and it was still one of the best sundogs he'd ever been able to photograph, as the light had been elongated by a nearby cloud, making it look like a short flat rainbow instead of the typical round sundog.

The calendar had been a Christmas gift from Wilma Jean, who had secretly collected 12 of what she'd considered to be his best photos and sent them off to a company that would turn them into calendars and postcards.

Other months included photos of Hoppie and Pierre playing in the ditch, Bud on the tractor (taken by Wilma Jean), a couple of spectacular sunsets over the Reef, and the purple lilac bush in bloom in the backyard, as well as one of Wilma Jean and her cousin Juno in front of the Airstream. And she had of course included the picture of the train that he'd won the ribbon for at the Price Fair, making sure a photo of the ribbon was included on that page.

She'd titled the calendar, "The Best of Bud," which was printed on the front, as well as at the bottom of each page, and he knew she'd sent copies to a number of friends and relatives, including his old high-school teacher Mrs. Martin, who had said he'd never amount to anything if he didn't apply himself a little more.

Mrs. Martin was now a resident down in the Beehive House in Loa, and Wilma Jean said she knew she would enjoy hearing from one of her old students.

Bud didn't consider the photos anything even close to his best, but he knew she'd collected them more along the lines of her own interests, so he'd let it go lest he seemed unappreciative.

He had much better ones—for example, the one he'd taken from the top of Rooster Hill as Amtrak passed below, the entire train lit up like a silver cannonball streaking through town. He'd set his camera to a real slow shutter speed to get that one.

And how about the one of the purple lupine all backlit by afternoon light? That one was taken by the bank building, as he'd noticed it in their planter while waiting at the drive-through to deposit his paycheck. He'd leaned out the window using his telephoto while Junkyard Goldie sat behind him in his truck, honking. He was really proud of how he'd blurred the background behind the flower in what he later learned photographers called bokeh.

Now remembering why he was looking at the calendar in the first place, Bud noted it was only two days until the summer solstice. He felt a moment of panic. He needed to get ahold of Howie and find out how serious he was about finding Mackie's treasure, for he had a feeling he wasn't the only one who had figured it out.

Bud crawled back under the tractor, deciding to finish up and then go call Howie. He felt like he'd kind of dropped the ball on the couple in the Ford LTD and was wondering if they'd managed to get a ride out to get their car.

Bud put a few bolts back in place, then slid out from beneath the tractor. Had he even told Howie the couple was Angus's next of kin, the ones he'd been trying to contact down in St. George? He couldn't remember, but didn't think he had. Had he really dropped the ball that badly?

He went and sat down in the old gray office chair in the corner of the shop, the one he used to scoot around on when working on things.

He was beginning to realize that finding Angus Mackie had affected him more than he'd thought. He knew he'd wanted to get away from it all, but it had been a somewhat vague feeling, and he hadn't really connected it to the old Scotsman's death until just now.

Things had seemed hectic and even out of control, which had made him decide to go out with Eldon and Frosty, but he was just now realizing how the old man's death, combined with Wilma Jean wanting to sell everything, had really affected his equilibrium.

Add to that all the strange going-ons with so-called spacemen and also including Duncan and his family, and it was no wonder Bud felt discombobulated. The weird dream he'd had the previous night was just icing on the cake.

It was no wonder he was forgetting to tell Howie important stuff, even though it really wasn't his responsibility, and he knew Howie didn't intend to make him feel like it was. It seemed like Howie leaned on Bud because he was still somewhat of a rookie, combined with the fact that he worked alone. Maybe Bud should go to the mayor and see if he could influence him to hire a deputy, like Howie wanted.

Just then, Bud's phone rang.

"Yell-ow," he answered, wiping his hands on his grease rag.

It was Wilma Jean.

"Hon, I just wanted to let you know that the man I mentioned who's leasing a booth is here now in case you want to come down. It looks like he has some good stuff."

"Thanks, but I'm covered with grease," Bud answered. "Maybe I can make it down later."

"That's fine," she replied. "But if you see any of your friends, tell them he has folding camp shovels. They probably won't last very long."

"Sounds good. Is he getting a lot of people to take his survey?"

"He is, and he's also giving out toasters. But hon, if you come down, don't be mad at me, OK?"

"Why would I be mad?" Bud asked.

"Well, I didn't want him to disrupt things too much by sitting close to the front, so I put him in your back booth. It's only for a few days, hon."

Bud was silent for a moment, then said, "It's OK. I need to get used to not having my pick of booths for when you sell the cafe. But I think maybe I'll come on down after all and get one of those shovels."

Bud stuck his grease rag in the back pocket of his coveralls and walked out the shop door. He had a hunch that Howie would also show up at the cafe, and he needed to talk to him.

28

"Sheriff, you look like you just got out of jail in that striped suit," Howie grinned, eyeing Bud's coveralls. He then added, "I hope the cafe proprietor doesn't mind a little grease on her booth seat. But you'll have to wait your turn for one of those shovels. Where you been, anyway?"

Bud sat down in the booth across from Howie, not at all surprised to find him there.

"I had a lapse in continuity," Bud replied.

"What does that mean?" Howie asked.

"I went down to June's Bottom with the BOB-O's. I tried to call you about the people in the Ford LTD."

"People in the Ford LTD?" Howie asked, perplexed.

"You mean they didn't call you to help them get their car unstuck?"

"No," Howie said. "Nobody called me, except Lily Coleman."

"What did she want?" Bud asked, knowing Lily worked at the River Museum.

"Well," Howie replied. "She wanted me to go check on a vehicle parked by the watermelon float out on the far side of the parking lot.

She said someone was messing around out by the John Wesley Powell statue."

"Did you find anything?"

"I did. It turned out some tourists were looking for a geocache someone had put there. I helped them find it. Now that's a hobby I could actually get into, Bud."

Bud grinned as Maureen set a cup of coffee in front of him and asked, "Ice cream?"

Bud, knowing Wilma Jean was in the back, replied, "No, maybe just some half-and-half."

Maureen laughed. "Wilma Jean went to the bank." She placed a small dish of vanilla ice cream on the table.

Putting a dollop in his coffee, Bud sat back and asked, "Howie, how long have you been waiting here to do a survey?"

"Not too long," Howie replied. "Since there's two of them back there right now, it's taking a little longer."

Bud looked to the back booth, where he saw a sign that read, "Free Survey. Earn a Toaster or Camp Shovel in 10 Minutes. Easy and No Obligation."

He could make out two people, heads bent, filling out surveys. He wasn't sure, but it looked like Mackie's nephew Graham and his wife Clara. A man sat across from them, but all Bud could see was the back of his head.

"Howie," Bud whispered. "Don't look now, but it's the people with the Ford LTD."

"Ford LTD? You mean the ones you said were supposed to call me?"

"Yes," Bud said. "Howie, listen to me. I gave them a ride back the other day from out in the desert. They were stuck. I took them to the Robber's Roost Motel, and they were going to call you. I tried to call you later, but you didn't answer, and then I went out with the BOB-O's and forgot all about it."

"Was it something important, Sheriff?" Howie asked.

"Considering who they are, I think so," Bud replied. "Their names are Graham and Clara Mackie. They're Mackie's next of kin from St. George."

"How did they know to come up here?" Howie asked. "I never got ahold of them."

"They were already here, Howie," Bud whispered. "They had the old man out with them camping, said he wanted to revisit his old haunts, and he got lost. They were supposed to call you."

Howie now looked upset. "Bud, you really dropped the ball on this one. How long ago was all this?"

"A couple of days ago."

"Do you think I should call Radium SAR? Is it too late to look for him?"

Bud sighed. "Howie, no point in looking for him. He's dead. We already found him."

"Oh man," Howie replied. "I'm losing track of things, too. We need to tell them so they can go get his ashes."

"We do, Howie, but I didn't want to spill the beans before talking to you, in case you had questions for them."

"What kind of questions should I ask them, Bud?"

"I'm not sure, Howie. Maybe it's just time to tell them and not worry about who's guilty for now, if anyone is."

Just then, the couple stood, picked up two folding shovels, then walked through the cafe.

"Next," said the man administering the survey, turning to see who was there.

Bud was surprised to see it was Lieutenant Esker. He was a psychologist working for the Health Service? Maybe he was just moonlighting, Bud thought.

Now Graham and Clara walked by, and seeing Bud, stopped. Bud noted that Clara's hair was no longer in curlers, but instead fell in tight ringlets from her head.

Graham said, "We sure wanted these shovels, given what happened with us getting stuck. Thanks again for helping us the other day. Is this the sheriff we were supposed to call?" He nodded at Howie.

"Yes," Bud answered. "This is Sheriff Howie McPhearson. Sheriff, this is Graham and Clara Mackie."

Howie said, "Nice to meet you." Bud could tell Howie was anxious to take the survey before anyone else came in.

Slipping from the booth, Bud asked Graham and Clara, "Can I talk to you for a minute outside?"

"Do you need me to come along?" Howie asked.

"No, go ahead and do the survey," Bud replied, following the pair out the cafe door.

Graham asked, "Is there something you want to talk about? Oh, wait, I know. I forgot to pay you back the money I borrowed."

Graham handed Bud the money then added, "That was still one of the nicer things anyone's done for us, complete strangers like that. We got a ride back out from the guy who owns the motel. But here, let me add some extra so you can get yourself a sandwich and some coffee at the cafe here."

"It's OK," Bud replied. "I get free food here—my wife owns it. But what I wanted to ask you—did you ever talk to anyone about your Uncle Angus, you know, with him missing and all?"

Now Graham and Clara both looked sad, and Clara replied, "We just got back from Price with his ashes today. Very tragic."

Bud was surprised. "His ashes? How did you know to go get them, I mean, that he'd passed?"

"We're going to have a service out where he died," Graham said. "I'm going to play the pipes. You're invited, you know. We'll let you know when it is."

"The pipes?" Bud asked.

"Yes," Clara said. You know, bagpipes. Graham's a piper, just like his Uncle Angus was."

Bud was stymied. How did they know where Angus had died? Were they complicit somehow? If so, they sure weren't trying to hide anything.

"Did you talk to the sheriff?" Bud tried again.

Graham replied, "No, no, but we did talk to the coroner, and he told us Angus had fallen and hit his head. Very sad way to go, but at least it was quick. We both feel terrible. If only he hadn't wandered off..."

How had they known Angus was dead, yet alone that the ambulance had taken his body to Price? He knew Howie hadn't told them —he didn't even know them until Bud introduced them a few moments ago. And as far as Bud knew, he and Howie were the only ones who knew, other than the coroner and mortician.

Bud tried one last time. "Who told you Angus was dead and where his body was found?"

"Oh, that's easy. It was Duncan. You know him, he was staying out at your place. But we have to go, Mr. Shumway. We want to go visit the museum."

"Duncan?" Bud felt like he needed a good long nap—he must still be sleep deprived for things to be this confusing.

"Are you going back to St. George now?" Bud asked.

"No," replied Graham."We're committed to finding my uncle's treasure. We'll be staying at the motel for a few days. But thanks again for everything. We'll be in touch for the service."

They walked down the sidewalk towards the museum, leaving Bud feeling like all he wanted to do was go back to the farm and crawl back under that big John Deere tractor.

29

"I thought you were going to get a camp shovel," Howie said, leaning against the tractor as Bud worked beneath it.

Bud replied, "Howie, I had to get back to work. Besides, I don't need one. I already have at least two folding camp shovels."

"Then why were you there?" Howie asked.

"I was going to get one for you. I just wanted to check it all out, since it's at the cafe."

"That was nice of you," Howie said. "Now *I* have two camp shovels. The only thing I don't like is that it has 'Property of U.S. Army' stenciled on it. I'm going to put it in Maureen's VW Bug."

"Good idea." Bud crawled out from under the tractor and stood, again wiping his hands on the grease rag.

Howie added, "Man, those shovels were really popular. Old Man Green and Frosty and Eldon all got one. The toasters didn't seem to be much of a hit, though."

"Howie, what was on that survey you took, anyway?"

"That survey? Oh, man, Bud, that was really off the wall. It asked how long I'd been in Green River, and how old I was, and if I was married, that kind of stuff, then it went right into bizarro world."

"Bizarro world?"

"Yeah, it asked me if I'd ever seen a UFO or alien, and if so, was I scared, and a bunch of stuff like that. But the final question was a real humdinger. It asked how I would react if the President announced there were aliens among us."

"What did you say?"

"I wrote that I would personally like to meet them, because I have a few questions for them."

Bud laughed. "What kind of questions?"

"Well, for example, I want to know why they've been messing with us for so long, pretending they exist, then they don't, then they do. And I want to know how they can travel long distances without taking forever. Stuff like that. But I did tell the guy administering the survey that his terminology was all wrong. Like everyone else, he had spacemen and aliens confused."

Bud took a long drink of water from his water jug, then asked, "Howie, not to change the subject, but did you possibly mention Angus Mackie's death to anyone, even Maureen?"

Howie shook his head no. "I would never do that. She knows my work can be confidential, Bud."

"Well, how in hellsbells could Graham and Clara know all the details—they knew Angus was dead and up in Price, and they talked to the coroner. They told me Duncan told them, but how could he have known?"

"Maybe he was nearby when it all came down, Bud. That's the only way I can think of that he would know."

"I agree, Howie. And that means he knew what was going on. Yet he told me just last night that he was going to look for Angus until he found him."

"And you haven't seen him since?"

"No. He was asleep when I went out to the trailer this morning, and Wilma Jean said when she saw him at breakfast that he told her he was going to start camping in his plane, now that he had it back. It's almost as if he's avoiding me. And yet Graham and Clara went to Price just today. How would he know to tell them to go up there?"

"Well," Howie replied, "He either found out today where Angus was and told them, or he already knew and was trying to throw you off. Do you think he may have killed his own grandfather, Bud?"

Bud sat down in the office chair and started slowly rolling it back and forth. He wished he had the rose quartz to fiddle with, but it was home in his shirt pocket. It was hard to think without fiddling.

"He doesn't seem like the type at all, Howie. But something odd— it seemed like Graham and Clara were looking for Duncan when I first met him, and they had Angus with them. He actually hid under my FJ. Why would he be hiding from his family then, and yet now they're all friendly?"

"I dunno, Bud. Maybe they're going to band together now to find the treasure."

"Well," Bud replied. "There's another actor in all this drama, a guy named Ryder Gates. He drives a tan Jeep, and he told me he's been looking for Angus's treasure for 10 years, and that Angus was a liar and thief. I have no idea what that's all about, but he struck me as somewhat of a shady character, kind of like a repo man."

"Howie now sighed, leaning against the big tractor. "Bud," he said. "You're driving me nuts with all that rolling back and forth in that darn chair."

Bud stood up, looking apologetic.

Howie now said, "I'm beginning to see how you burned out on this job. It's all making me want to just go play music. Howie and the Ramblin' Road Rangers needs to start making some money so I can do what you did and change professions. Anyone with an ant's rear-end worth of sense could see they don't pay enough for all this worry and stress, and every time I talk to the mayor, he just says to deputize you when I need help and have you send him the bill."

Bud replied, "He couldn't begin to afford all the hours I've put into this case, especially if you count when I'm sleeping—or trying to. But Howie, let's talk about something else for awhile. I'm tired of trying to think."

"I got an emergency call today, we could talk about that," Howie offered.

"What happened?" Bud asked.

"Well, the call came in, and I first heard someone say, 'There's no reception here,' then I heard that guy and someone else start talking about waders. Before long, they'd progressed to discussing how much fun it would be to hop a freight, then they talked about how you can use a flathead screwdriver to hotwire a car, then they started discussing a certain pretty gal who worked down at the Melon Rind, wondering if she was married. It was at that point that I figured out it was Marv Lyons and Corky Meyers down at the Palatial Estates Trailer Park, and since they were tying up the emergency line, I drove down there and informed them that their engines were running but there wasn't anybody on board."

Bud laughed. "Were they discussing Maureen?"

"I'm not sure. It could've been Wilma Jean."

Bud frowned as Howie continued, "Is she about to get her license Bud? I've seen her flying a few times. That's sure a humdinger of a little plane Vern's got out at the airport."

"Well," Bud answered. "I think she has a ways to go. I sure hope she can buy the plane, though. But say, Howie, are you still interested in finding Mackie's treasure?"

"Of course I am. You have any ideas?"

"Actually, I do. Do you have the poem with you?"

"No, but I have it memorized."

"Quote me the part about the man in the scree."

Howie said:

> It's not a place where one walks free,
> But if you search at setting sun,
> You'll see the man high in the scree,
> His left arm points where search is done.

Bud said, "Howie, I think I know where the treasure is. I can show you where, but it's not going to be easy to get to. But we have only two days to get it all done. We need to be out at the canyons at sundown day after tomorrow, because it's only on solstice when the clue appears. You'll need to get a jetboat and someone who can take you down the river opposite June's Bottom. I can't go because I'll be showing you where to look."

"I'm game," Howie said. "But Bud, that really doesn't make sense that you can't go because you'll be showing me where to look."

"I have to stand on the rim and tell you where to look as the clue is revealed, and it's going to get dark shortly thereafter. We'll need walkie-talkies with a good range, as cell phones won't be reliable down in there. You'll also need a good light and a good boatman to take you back upriver. It could be risky, especially if anyone else has figured it out. I think you need to get someone you trust to go with you, maybe even a couple of people, and you'll want to be armed. Are you sure you want to do this?"

Howie thought for a moment then replied, "I'm sure, Bud. We can split the treasure, or you can have as much of it as you want, since you have it all figured out."

"Howie," Bud replied. "I'm not a bit worried about that, because I'm not sure it's worth one red cent. Didn't Angus call it fool's gold? It very well could be, and we'll see how many other fools have figured it out, assuming you still want to look for it, not that I'm calling you a fool."

Howie thought for a minute, then said, "I still want to go look, Bud. It might be worthless, but if it's not, it could make a big difference in both of our lives. I don't mind playing the fool, just in case. Bud, do you think others have figured it out?"

"Probably not," Bud replied. "You have to be in the exact right place at the exact right time, and it only happens once a year at summer solstice. Only someone who's been in this country a lot has the odds in their favor of ever seeing it, and then it's a slim chance. Angus was out there, and he probably just happened to be lucky to see it, like I was."

Howie replied, "Well, whatever happens, it'll make a good story if nothing else, right, Sheriff?"

"I hope so," Bud replied, thinking of Ryder Gates and wondering if he'd been out in the canyons looking for Mackie's treasure long enough to know what was going on.

30

Bud really preferred to sit in the back of the plane, even though he knew he could get better photos from the front seat. Both Wilma Jean and Vern had tried to talk him into sitting in front, but he felt Wilma Jean should sit there and get in some flying time.

It would count towards her hours, and Bud wasn't really here to get photos, anyway. Besides, he could better hide his trepidation in the back. No point in his wife knowing how nervous flying made him.

Vern's Cessna 150 bumped down the Green River Municipal Airport runway, and Bud was glad he was in the back so he couldn't see how close they were getting to the old highway. They were thankfully up and away before reaching it.

Bud hadn't really planned on doing any flying, but Vern had invited him to come along, since it was a beautiful day, and Bud figured they could maybe fly over Tumbleweed Geyser. Vern had said he knew where it was, which didn't surprise Bud any, as, like Eldon, Vern knew this country like the back of his hand.

Bud wished he'd thought of asking Vern about the geyser earlier, and when he'd shown Vern the list of initials, he'd been able to name every one:

C was Crystal; TM was Ten Mile; PTM was Pseudo Ten Mile; T

was Tumbleweed; TS was Torrey's Spring; BB was Big Bubbly; LB was Little Bubbly; SS was Side Seep; C/C was Champagne/Chaffin; and A was, of course, Airport.

Some of the geysers were on the other side of the river, over by Ten Mile Canyon, but Bud wasn't interested in seeing them, he mostly just wanted to fly over Tumbleweed, which Vern had said wasn't far from Chaffin Ranch.

Bud was surprised at how buttery smooth the plane now flew, and he leaned over to take a few photos as they gained altitude. He hoped they had plenty of gas, even though Vern had said it would be a short flight, as they would just follow the River Road.

Bud saw a Jeep on the road below and thought of Ryder. He hadn't seen hide nor hair of him since he'd come up from June's Bottom, and he was hoping he'd somehow found out that Angus was dead and had gone on home. No point in trying to follow someone who no longer existed.

Bud now thought of Duncan, wondering where he'd gone off to. His plane was at the airport, but Duncan hadn't appeared to be anywhere nearby. Maybe he was down at the Melon Rind taking the survey, Bud thought.

Now they were flying over Fossil Point, and Bud could make out a couple of vehicles parked there below the cliffs. It was a popular place for people wanting to see dinosaur bones, as the cliffs and rocks displayed them in situ, and a trail led around to the various locations.

"I'm flying now," Wilma Jean said over the headphones. "Get your parachutes ready!"

Bud knew she was joking, but he thought it might make him feel more comfortable if they actually did have parachutes, though how they would ever exit the small plane in time to deploy them was another matter.

Since he was sitting directly behind Vern, Bud could see the look of sheer delight and exuberance on his wife's face, and it was the first he began to understand how much flying meant to her. He decided he would do everything in his power to make sure they could buy Vern's little Piper Cub.

They were now over the Big Empty, and from the air, its red sands reminded Bud of Mars.

Now Vern said over the headphones, "We're almost to Tumbleweed Geyser. See how that wash kind of runs at an angle to the northeast? The geyser is right at the top of that angle. I'll circle it so you can get a photo. Looks like we have company."

Bud couldn't yet see the geyser, as it was dead-ahead of the plane, but Vern tipped the wings as he circled. Bud spotted a small reddish area with white around its perimeter, and he knew it was the travertine circling the geyser.

But what was interesting was that he could also see a car parked nearby, with three figures standing nearby.

"That's a rough road," Vern said. "I'm surprised they got a car in there. It has some places that are high clearance."

"Somebody with some good Army surplus shovels, I bet," Bud replied. "But could you circle again, maybe a little lower?"

The plane circled again, Vern dropping low enough that Bud could make out what kind of vehicle it was—sure enough, he saw that it was the white Ford LTD. The three figures waved at them.

"It's two men and a woman," Wilma Jean noted. "They're intrepid to drive a low-rider like that back in there. Maybe we should fly over on our way back to make sure they're not stuck."

Bud groaned. It was the Mackie crew, and he now knew where Duncan was. It wouldn't surprise him one bit to find out they were indeed stuck.

Vern now straightened out the plane, turning the controls back to Wilma Jean and saying, "Did you get what you needed, Bud? Want to circle again?"

"I'm fine," Bud replied. "Vern, do you think those geysers are all connected somehow?"

"I do," Vern replied. "I'm no geologist, but I know they're all somehow the result of drilling down through the Navajo Sandstone into a layer that holds carbon dioxide. The sandstone keeps it in place until someone punctures a hole in it, then the carbon dioxide can come up when the pressure builds up. This whole area was once a big sandy desert with giant dunes that through time were compressed by various forces into sandstone. You go over to the east around Cisco, and that's all a huge Army Reserve for helium, which is a really rare gas. It's all being held down there just like the carbon dioxide until someone drills through the sandstone."

"So," Bud asked, "Are all these geysers around the same depth?"

"I would assume so, Bud," Vern answered. "But who knows? I do know that Crystal Geyser is now a mere shade of itself. When I was a kid, it used to spout up almost 70 or 80 feet, and now it barely even goes off. People have filled the bore hole with rocks."

"Why would they do that?" Wilma Jean asked.

"I don't know," Vern replied. "Unless they think throwing a rock down the pipe will trigger it to go off. They're ruining it. Someday they'll have to re-drill it if the town wants it to be a tourist attraction."

They were now flying to the northeast and about to cross the Green River when Bud asked, "Say, would it be possible to fly down past Trin-Alcove Bend and over June's Bottom?"

"Sure," Vern replied, banking the plane to the south and following the river. They were soon over the big alfalfa fields of Ruby Ranch, then the remnants of the Chaffin Ranch where the San Rafael River flowed into the Green.

The river snaked below them, gradually dropping into a deep canyon, and they soon came to a place where it made a huge bend at least a thousand feet below the white sandstone rim.

"We're coming to Trin-Alcove Bend," Vern said, cutting the engine speed and slowing the plane. "This is where Three Canyon comes in."

"Why's it called that?" asked Wilma Jean.

"There are three deep canyons that meet the Green after merging into one drainage just above the river. In his diaries, John Wesley Powell talks about the three canyons merging together and being so tortuous and steep that they looked like alcoves from below. That's why he named it Trin Alcove."

They were now over the tight bend, which formed a U in the river beneath sheer cliffs. The sandstone neck in the middle was so narrow that Bud knew it was just a matter of time before the river cut through it, leaving an abandoned meander, or rincon, like the one at Anderson Bottom.

"Look!" he said. "There's a road coming in from the west side to the edge of the cliff right across from June's Bottom."

"That comes in from over by the Ruby Ranch Road," Vern replied. "Looks like there's someone standing out on the edge."

Bud could now see a tan Jeep below and figured he knew who that someone might be.

As they flew over, the figure got down on its stomach and crawled as far out on the edge as possible, as if trying to scope out the landscape below.

"You're a few hundred feet off," Bud thought, a knot suddenly tightening in his stomach.

"But not far enough off that you won't soon figure it out, if you're who I think you are."

31

Bud was craving spanakopita, but he knew it was a hopeless enterprise, as there was no way he was going to drive to the Greek Streak just to appease his stomach. He was beginning to wonder if one's stomach could get sundowners, as his sure seemed to always crave something or other around sundown and would take him out and about if he'd let it.

He went into the kitchen and looked in the fridge, but didn't see anything that looked good—it hadn't been all that long since he'd had a tuna sandwich at the Melon Rind, and he knew he was just being habitual and wasn't even hungry. There was still strawberry ice cream in the freezer, but it just didn't sound good. Maybe he was burning out on ice cream, he hoped, as it sure would make life easier.

Thinking for a moment—WWWJD?—What Would Wilma Jean Do?—he made himself a cup of tea, taking it back into the living room and sitting down in his recliner, laptop at hand, the dogs at his feet.

He downloaded the photos he'd taken that morning while out flying with Vern and Wilma Jean, now wishing he'd gone ahead and sat in the front. Fortunately, most of them had turned out fine, and he enjoyed recreating the flight visually—Fossil Point, Tumbleweed Geyser, the river itself, Trin-Alcove Bend, and June's Bottom.

He zoomed in on the photo of Tumbleweed Geyser to where he could confirm that, sure enough, it was indeed the Ford LTD, and he could make out Duncan standing next to Graham and Clara. What were they doing there? And what was the significance of Tumbleweed Geyser on Duncan's map? He felt no closer to solving the mystery than he'd been before.

Bud next brought up the photo of the tan Jeep on the rim of Trin Alcove Bend and studied it closely. He zoomed in as far as he could, and it did indeed look like Ryder, though he wasn't 100-percent certain. Whoever it was, they were dangerously close to the edge.

Now on the Internet, he did a search on Trin-Alcove Bend. He brought up several boater's webpages where they'd floated down Labyrinth Canyon, as that stretch of river was called, and even found some photos of June's Bottom and Three Canyon, then finally came across the journals of John Wesley Powell.

Powell and his crew had been the earliest non-native explorers of the canyons in 1869, and Powell kept extensive journals of his trip in his book, *The Exploration of the Colorado River and its Canyons*. Bud soon found an entry for Trin Alcove Bend:

July 15: Our camp is in a great bend of the canyon. The curve is to the west and we are on the east side of the river. Just opposite, a little stream comes down through a narrow side canyon. We cross and go up to explore it. At its mouth another lateral canyon enters, in the angle between the former and the main canyon above. Still another enters in the angle between the canyon below and the side canyon first mentioned; so that three side canyons enter at the same point. These canyons are very tortuous, almost closed in from view, and, seen from the opposite side of the river, they appear like three alcoves. We name this Trin-Alcove Bend.

Bud loved to read about the history of the canyons and had almost gone down that rabbit hole, reading along in Powell's diary, when he remembered his pending order for a wide-angle camera lens, something he dearly needed if he was going to get into night-sky photography.

He went back to the on-line store and clicked on the "One-Click Order Button," a surge of happiness coursing through him, which he knew deep inside was actually just dopamine and would soon subside, at least until the lens arrived.

But as he studied the screen to see when the lens would be shipped, he noticed he'd ordered the wrong one. Instead of the 24mm wide-angle lens he needed for star shots, he'd accidentally ordered a 100mm macro lens instead, one he'd put into his cart earlier and forgotten.

Both lenses were equally expensive, and Bud now felt the dopamine quickly subside and turn into anxiety. He actually preferred the 24mm lens, but he'd also wanted a good macro lens for shooting close-ups of flowers and insects. He really should cancel the macro, as he couldn't afford both.

Now, from nowhere, three separate thoughts crowded into his brain: what Howie had said about him becoming a professional photographer; how nice the photo of the lupine by the bank had turned out; and the words of his favorite artist, Bob Ross, who always said there were no mistakes, only happy accidents.

Bud quickly put the 24mm lens into his shopping cart, again pressed the "One-Click Order Button," and jumped up and went out to the back porch before he could register what he'd just done.

He started pacing, then remembered the rose quartz in his pocket and took it out, feeling a sense of relief as he sat in the porch swing, fiddling with it.

He could justify buying both lenses, and he knew Wilma Jean wouldn't mind, especially since she was getting ready to buy an airplane. Actually, this would be a good time to buy that new camera, Bud thought, impetuously going back inside.

He'd soon pressed the "One-Click Order Button" for the third time, ordering a high-resolution full-frame camera, the one the pros used and that he'd wanted for a long time, adrenaline now coursing through his veins along with the dopamine.

Back on the porch swing, suddenly feeling subdued, Bud again took the rock from his pocket, noting he'd worn off even more travertine.

He was getting really fond of the rock—it was the best fiddling device he'd had so far, as it was easy to conceal in his pocket, and if Wilma Jean did see him fiddling with it, he could say he was trying to wear off the travertine so he could make her a necklace with it.

He now stood and began pacing back and forth, little Pierre grabbing his pant leg and dragging along, Bud so distracted he didn't even notice.

He was again trying to justify his big purchase when he realized he'd never checked to see whose debit card was on the account. Rushing back inside, he checked, only to find it was Wilma Jean's. What if she didn't have enough cash in her account to pay for everything?

He would just have to go to the bank and cover it first thing tomorrow when they opened, he figured, but there would now be no way he could fudge on what it was costing, as she would know. But he needed to keep that airplane purchase in mind, he told himself, sighing as he sat back in the porch swing, Pierre still dragging along on his pant leg.

As Bud sat there, his emotions vacillating between the excitement of finally getting the equipment he'd been wanting and the dread of having spent that much money, he didn't even notice the white figure approaching the back gate until the dogs started barking.

Looking up, he saw yet another spaceman, and his first thought was that it wanted him to help it remove its helmet.

"You guys need to invent a helmet-removal mechanism," Bud said to the figure.

"I'm here to see if you'll take my survey," it replied. "I have a shovel for you. Can I come into the yard?"

32

Lieutenant Walt Esker sat across from Bud in the living room, drinking tea, his spaceman helmet on the couch next to him, the dogs eyeing it as if it were something from outer space.

"I actually wanted to stop by and thank you and your wife for helping me out," he said. "Is she at the cafe?"

"No, she's at the bowling alley," Bud replied. "She won't be home until late, but I'll be sure she knows. Don't you have a couple of more days of surveys to do?"

"No, I ran out of shovels," Walt replied. "And nobody wants toasters. Do you guys need one?"

"Sure," Bud replied. "I can put it out in the Airstream."

"I'll get one out of my car when I go," Walt said.

"Are you leaving Green River? Is your mission accomplished?" Bud asked.

"Pretty much," Walt replied.

"Are you going to wear that spacesuit on the road?"

Walt laughed. "Actually, I put it on thinking I'd get a selfie with you and your wife. Kind of a remembrance of the experiment."

"Experiment?"

"Yes, I think it's safe to tell you now what we've been doing."

"I thought it was a top secret investigation of all the spacemen hanging around out here," Bud said wryly.

"You were obviously on to us," Walt said. "How did you know?"

"All I know is that real spacemen probably wouldn't be running around in those silly suits, especially if they wanted to roast hot dogs."

"Well," Walt replied. "I'm sorry I couldn't be forthright with you. We wanted to go with the stereotype so there would be no question about things. We wanted to be sure people knew they were seeing spacemen. It may seem silly, but it's actually a very serious study. We're talking potential public safety."

"You're not going to tell me those weren't real spacemen out and about?" Bud kidded.

"Well, Bud, who knows for sure? But the ones around here were U.S. Army soldiers."

"I would expect the Air Force to be involved if it's spacemen," Bud replied.

"The old missile base is an army holding. Both the Army and Air Force were involved in the old missile project. But the Army is studying potential terrestrial threats, which is what an alien invasion would be."

"Are we being invaded?" Bud asked, puzzled. "By non-Army spacemen, I mean."

"Well, not as far as we know, but it could happen. This project was set up to gauge how people would respond to such an invasion so we can handle it properly if we ever are."

"Are you telling me this was a big psychological experiment by the U.S. Army on behalf of the American citizen and Joe Q. Public? Scaring everyone to death and using our tax monies to pay for it?"

"Yes."

"In the name of national security?"

"I take it you don't believe in UFOs," Walt asked.

"I don't, but if I ever see one, I will. But why Green River?"

"Well, first of all, there's the base, and even though it's all just ruins at this time, it did give us a place for our headquarters."

"You've been out there all this time with the rattlers and rabbits?"

"There are rattlesnakes out there?"

"A few," Bud replied.

"Well," Walt continued. "Green River had the missile base here for over a decade, and most of the guys who worked there lived here. And even though that was awhile ago, we figured the people here would be more likely to not panic if there were strange things going on."

"There have been strange things going on here since the town was founded in the late 1800s and nobody's panicked yet," Bud grinned. "Spacemen aren't a big deal at all compared to some of it."

"Well, the town actually did seem to take it pretty much in stride, except for that one old farmer who started shooting at us."

"That would be Old Man Green," Bud replied. "He actually came in and took your survey—he wanted a shovel."

Walt laughed. "I remember him. He's the one who said if the President announced there were aliens among us he'd just shoot them all."

"He probably would, too," Bud said. "Especially if he'd been drinking his homemade hard cider. But what exactly was this study supposed to show?"

"Well, that's pretty much classified. But you probably figured out I'm actually a psychologist with the Army. This study is an attempt to predict the psychological reactions to extraterrestrials in a systematic way, which has never been done. We're generally finding that the reaction seems to be much more positive than negative."

"You mean, you scare the bejeebers out of people, like when you asked me and Howie to leave, and still get a positive response?"

"I'm not sure about that one," Walt replied. "What happened?"

"Nothing really," Bud answered. "A spaceman asked us to leave so he could get to work. But are you done with your study now?"

"No, we're actually just getting started. We want a sample of at least 500 people, so we're going to some other towns after this."

"Is Roswell on the list?" Bud asked.

"I can't answer that," Walt said. "Though you're on the right track.

But do you mind if I take that selfie now? I need to get back to the base."

Walt proceeded to put his helmet back on and take several photos with his arm around Bud's shoulder.

Bud then asked, "Do you mind if I take a couple, too?"

"Sure."

Bud first took a selfie with the spaceman's arm around his shoulder, then one of the spaceman pointing an egg-beater at him like a ray gun while Bud held his hands up, then a final one of Hoppie and Pierre supposedly running Walt off as he shuffled his feet.

Finally, as Walt again took off his helmet and prepared to leave, Bud asked, "Can you do me one last favor?"

"Sure," Walt replied.

"If you see the sheriff, put that helmet on real quick and wave at him."

"I can do that," Walt grinned.

He then handed Bud a toaster, got into his car, and disappeared into the dust, which vaguely reminded Bud of what aether might look like, the way it caught the moonlight's shimmer.

He wondered if Wilma Jean would use one of the photos he'd just taken on the next "Best of Bud" calendar, then sat down to order a nice carbon-fiber tripod to go with his new camera gear.

33

Bud sat in the back booth of the Melon Rind Cafe, noticing that the "For Sale" sign that had been in the window was now gone.

He was still somewhat in shock, as he'd just added up the price on his two new lenses, new camera body, and tripod, then deposited a check for that amount in Wilma Jean's bank account, taking it from his savings.

It had ended up being more than he'd spent on his first old car in high school, a pale green 1959 Chevy Bel-Air convertible with power glide two-speed automatic transmission. He wasn't sure if the value of the dollar had decreased or if the camera gear was overpriced—probably both, he suspected.

He was surprised at how busy the cafe was, as the usual breakfast crowd was long gone since it was now mid-morning. He looked around and saw no one he recognized, which was unheard of. Must be treasure hunters, he thought, feeling a sort of high energy in the air.

It was then that he remembered it was the solstice. Had everyone figured out what was going on? He thought back on the treasure poem.

So do it now, and if you fail,
You know your life will be at stake,
For June it is, you've heard the tale,
And summer solstice is the take.

Surely others had realized that whatever it was, it was going to happen on the solstice and this would be the day to "take" the treasure.

He now panicked. Where was Howie? Hadn't he said he wanted to go find the treasure? He should have a jetboat and crew arranged and be coordinating with him by now, Bud thought. They would need to head down the river by early afternoon.

Wilma Jean sat down in the booth opposite him. "Hon," she said. "You probably noticed I took the sign down. I've decided not to sell the cafe until the bowling alley sells."

"That makes sense," Bud replied. "But I just went to the bank. Don't be surprised to see a significant withdrawal from your account, but I just replaced it."

"Why would you withdraw money just to replace it?" she asked.

"I didn't. I bought some new camera gear and thought it was on my card, but it was on yours."

"New gear? You mean that little point and shoot I got you when we were in Radium wasn't good enough?"

Bud thought she was kidding, but he wasn't sure.

"And then I got you that nice body with the interchangeable lenses at the thrift shop, that old Pentax? Is this going to be the kind of thing where you're just never happy?"

"Kind of like wanting an airplane," Bud replied, still not sure if she was teasing or not. "I bet you get that little Piper Cub, then it won't be but a week or two until you'll want a Top Cub, right?"

"How do you know about Top Cubs?" she asked with surprise. "That's an airplane I would love to have, but only after I become a millionaire."

"Sammy mentioned it," Bud said, now again thinking about

Howie and wondering if maybe there weren't actually treasure out there after all.

Maybe he should call him. It would be nice to get Wilma Jean a Top Cub, even though they cost a cool quarter-million dollars. And he could use a star-tracker setup for shooting deep-sky night photos, the kind where you photograph nebulae and comets and such through a telescope.

Wilma Jean's voice brought him back from his reverie.

"I went flying with Vern for an hour this morning," she said, noticing Bud was now fiddling with the rose quartz. "I thought of you as we flew over Fiddler's Butte, hon. I couldn't believe all the vehicles out in the desert. Is something going on?"

Bud nodded his head towards the full cafe. "Treasure hunters," he said.

"Craziness," she replied. "But I gotta get back to it. I won't be home until late, as usual. Can you take the dogs out to the farm with you? I hope the bowling alley sells soon, hon. I'm getting worn out."

She stood and squeezed Bud's shoulder, then went back into the kitchen.

Bud now watched as a man entered the cafe, stood for a minute looking for a place to sit in the busy room, then came to the back and asked Bud if he could share his booth until a table opened up.

Bud nodded his head yes as Ryder Gates sat down across from him.

"Nice seeing you again," Bud said, feeling like a liar.

"Same," Ryder replied.

"Did you have a good time down on June's Bottom?" Bud asked, sipping the coffee Maureen had just set in front of him.

Ryder looked surprised. He hesitated, then said, "You sure run around with a weird bunch of characters."

"At least none of them eavesdrop," Bud replied.

Now Ryder looked pained. "I'm simply trying to return a stolen object to its rightful owner."

"And you thought maybe one of us stole it?"

"Of course not," said Ryder. "Coffee, please," he said as Maureen looked at him questioningly, having returned with Bud's ice cream.

Ryder continued, "I just thought you might know something about it."

"Why would any of us know anything?" Bud asked. "If you're looking for Mackie's treasure, I think you know exactly where it is."

Ryder looked surprised. "How would I know something like that?"

"Because the old man told you," Bud replied.

"Have you been talking to Angus?" Ryder asked.

"Not lately. But he either told you where to look or you guessed it on your own. And if you've been following him around for 10 years, I would guess that you know about the thing on the cliffs. He either told you or you saw it, correct?"

Ryder studied his coffee cup, then said, "I don't know where it is exactly, but I do have an idea. Have you seen it?"

"Yes, I have. I saw it a year ago to the day."

"On the solstice?"

"Yes. That's the only time it's visible," Bud replied.

"Would you like to have a partner?" Ryder asked.

"No thanks," Bud replied. "I already have one, though right now he's missing in action. But you were real close out there on the rim."

"How would you know?" Ryder asked.

"I was in that plane above you yesterday. You can find the strongbox on your own this evening—assuming nobody else beats you to it."

Ryder looked around the cafe, then said softly, "You know, that treasure is rightfully mine. Mackie swindled me."

"How so?" Bud asked.

"We went in together on an enterprise down in Australia. Mackie made a lot of money with his tire-pressure invention and he didn't need any more riches, but he's a prospector at heart. I heard about a lead down in Australia, and we went in as partners. He financed it all, of course, and I give him the credit for that, but it was my lead in the first place. All I got out of it was a few thousand dollars."

"It's none of my business," Bud said. "But how can you afford to follow him around for so long?"

Ryder shook his head. "I can't. But every time I catch up to him, he gives me a little more money so I can."

"So you can continue following him?" Bud was incredulous. "He gives you money so you can follow him around, looking for his treasure, trying to take it from him?"

"I guess so," Ryder said. "He always says the chase is good for both of us, keeps us on our toes."

"I thought you were his sworn enemy, his nemesis."

"I am, as much as one can be with a stubborn old Scot like that. I guess it's a love-hate relationship, mostly hate until I need money, then it's love, or maybe *like* would be a better word, or *tolerate* might be even better."

Maureen was now back to take their order. Ryder ordered a hamburger and baked beans, but Bud said he needed to get going.

Bud asked Ryder, "When was the last time you saw Angus?"

"Last time I saw him, he was in the nursing home down in St. George, a few weeks ago. He'd called me to come talk to him, but when I got there, he'd forgotten what he wanted to talk about. Neither of us is getting any younger. I told him he wanted to tell me where the treasure was, and he handed me a copy of that damn *Treasure Magazine*. He said his nephew, that guy Graham, was going to take him out there, and I should follow them around in case they found it, and then he wrote me a check for $10,000."

"Graham wrote you a check?" Bud asked.

"No, no, that guy can barely keep a shirt on his back. He drives an old junker car, and he and his wife are flat broke. He's too dumb to pour water out of a boot with the instructions written on the heel. Angus wrote me the check."

"And it was good?" Bud asked.

Ryder looked puzzled. "Of course it was good. Angus is a wealthy man, and that's because he's a liar and a cheat."

"I thought it was from inventing an automatic tire-pressure gauge," Bud replied.

"That, too," Ryder said. "Angus then told me his grandson, Duncan, helped him write that poem and knows where the treasure is, and I should follow him around if I wanted it. At that point, I decided either Angus was lying to me again or he'd lost it—probably both—'cause I can't follow him, Graham, and Duncan all around at the same time, especially since Angus gave his plane to Duncan."

Now Maureen brought his hamburger as Ryder added, "You can put your boots in the oven, but that don't make 'em biscuits. You can't change what the old man is. He's a liar and a cheat."

Bud stood to leave, saying, "Look, Ryder, it was nice talking to you, but I have to get back to work. Good luck this evening. Be careful if you're coming down from the top, it looks dangerous."

"Thanks. You have to be especially careful of witch's tongues," Ryder said, biting into his hamburger.

Bud walked out the door, thinking of his new camera and again wondering where Howie was, not even registering what Ryder had just said.

34

Bud drove by Howie and Maureen's big farm house, hoping to find Howie there, as Maureen had said it was his day off.

Bud had tried calling him, to no avail, and was wondering why he appeared to have totally forgotten about the fact that it was the solstice. It wasn't at all like him to not get back in touch with Bud, especially about something he'd shown such an interest in. Shoots, Bud thought, the whole thing was something Howie had wanted to pursue, not him.

Bud got out of his FJ, carrying the ice-cream maker under his arm, opened the gate, then stood on the front porch, ringing the doorbell.

Howie and Maureen had only been in the house for a couple of months, Bud noted, and they'd already fixed it up a lot. He especially liked the colorful baskets of flowers hanging from the covered porch alongside a half-dozen hummingbird feeders, all buzzing with activity.

Bud now knocked on the door, thinking maybe the doorbell wasn't working. When no one came, he walked around to the back— maybe Howie was out working in the back yard.

It was then he knew why Howie hadn't answered—it was because he couldn't hear him, not because the door bell didn't work. Howie apparently had his guitar amp turned up.

Bud listened as Howie played a riff or two, then started singing something about a two-timing gal who had two-timed him for the last two times and how he wasn't going to stand for it more than a couple of times more.

Bud laughed. It was good to hear Howie enjoying his music, for he knew it meant a lot to him. He thought again how Howie had said they were both artists and that maybe someday they could both pursue their art full time.

Bud wondered if that hadn't been partly what had influenced him to splurge on photography gear, at least subliminally, and even though it had never occurred to him that he might make a living someday from his photography, it was a nice thought. Maybe the day would come when he could get Wilma Jean to fly him to remote places where he could take unique landscape shots that some gallery would want to sell.

Bud grinned, now pounding on the door.

"Howie! Open up!"

He could hear guitar feedback, and Howie was soon at the door.

"Sheriff! Oh man, I was going to call you and I got all caught up in stuff. Come on in."

Bud went inside, handing Howie the ice-cream maker.

"This is a house-warming gift from me and Wilma Jean. We had to try it out, as we wanted to make sure it worked OK."

Howie grinned, "Good idea. Did it?"

"It's great. Try it with strawberries. But Howie, are we still on for this evening?"

Howie said, "Come on into the living room and have a seat, Sheriff. You want some iced tea?"

"No thanks," Bud said, sitting in Bodie's chair. "I just came from drinking too much coffee at the cafe. Where are Bodie and Tobie?"

"They're out playing in the barn," Howie said. "Though they wouldn't call it play, they're so serious. Chasing mice. But Bud, I'm really sorry I didn't get in touch with you. I'd like to say I forgot, but the truth is, I didn't."

"It's OK. What's going on?"

Howie looked conflicted, saying, "I've thought and thought about that treasure, Bud. I even got my metal detector all shined up and ready to go. I was pretty excited for awhile, but the more I thought about it, the less I wanted to get involved in something like that."

"I don't blame you one bit," Bud replied. "Especially if others are out there fighting over it."

"Do you think they will be?" Howie asked. "Could there be gunplay?"

"It's possible. I know for sure that guy Ryder's going to be out there tonight."

"Well, Bud," Howie said. "I'm plenty happy to get my treasure the honest way, by working for it. I was thinking about all the ramifications of finding a box of gold, assuming it's even real. First of all, we'd have to sell it, and that could be really hard. There are lots of scammers around. And since it's buried on government land, we might not even get to keep it after going to all that trouble. Then someone's going to want tax money. And everyone in Green River's going to think we're rich, and we know how that's going to shake out. First thing you know, Old Man Green's going to want us to open a bottling facility for his watermelon spritzer, hire a marketing team, do distribution, and all that. It's never going to end. Everyone in town's going to have something they really *really* need. I think I'd rather stay home and practice my guitar, since it's my day off."

Bud grinned. "Hey, Howie, guess what I did last night."

"I don't know. Take star photos?"

"You're close. I ordered a bunch of new photography gear. Wilma Jean's going to have a cow when she sees how much I spent, but I figured this was a good time—since she's buying an airplane, she can't say much."

"Might as well go ahead and sink the whole ship when you discover a small hole in the bottom, right Sheriff?" Howie grinned.

"Something like that," Bud replied.

"Well," Howie said. "You have to live life as best you can. You know, Sheriff, the more I get into my music, the more I realize that it's all about the road you take, not the destination. I mean, you need to choose your destination wisely, but there's no need to think about that and nothing else."

Howie sat down on Tobie's couch, then continued. "What life's really about is how you get there, the people you meet, the things you do that enrich your life and other peoples' lives, and who you become along the way. Treasure hunting really isn't something that has much of a journey to it, Bud, 'cause all you do is think about the destination, which is getting rich."

Bud was quiet for awhile, then said, "That's a really good way to put things, Howie, and I agree 100 percent. You know, in my life, I've found that the people who are doing the right thing aren't doing it because it will make them rich, they're doing it because it's the right thing. I've never been much of one for stuff like treasure hunting."

They both sat, silent, until Bud said, "You want to go on out to the rim anyway and see what happens on the solstice?"

"You bet," Howie said. "Let me put my guitar away and bring the cats in. Why don't you make us some sandwiches while I'm doing that—and there's some watermelon spritzer in the fridge, grab some of that. I'll be right back."

"It'll be a fun journey," Bud replied, not knowing they would soon find out otherwise.

35

Bud and Howie drove along the Airport Road in Bud's FJ, the sun slowly making its way down the western portion of its daily arc, turning the gray Mancos shales rich gold like fields of ripened wheat.

As they turned onto the River Road, dropping down to the red desert, Bud said, "Howie, we have plenty of time—let's swing over to Lover's Leap and take one last look at where we found Angus Mackie. You never know when something interesting might reveal itself."

"Good idea," Howie replied. "I sure wish we could figure out what happened. I've been asking around to try to find his grandson, but I can't seem to catch up to him. Do you think he's still in the area?"

"I saw him yesterday out at Tumbleweed Geyser," Bud replied.

"Where's that? Did you talk to him?"

"No, it was beneath me," Bud kidded. "I was flying with Vern and Wilma Jean. It's not too far from the river a few miles north of Chaffin Ranch."

Howie asked, "So, he's still around? Don't you think if he were guilty he'd be long gone? I guess that goes for the whole bunch of them—Mackie's relatives and that guy Ryder you mentioned."

"Well," Bud said. "It would make sense if there weren't a large sum of money involved. I think they're all still here because they want that treasure. If one of them did kill Mackie, they're willing to take their chances."

"If I'd done it, I'd be long gone, treasure or no," Howie replied as Bud turned off onto the road to Lover's Leap.

They bounced up the long grade that would take them to the rim above the river, the spot where Angus Mackie had died.

"I still can't figure out what a witch's tongue could be," Bud mused, slowing down for a rock that had fallen from the road cut. He pulled over, and Howie got out and moved it aside, then they continued on.

"It doesn't make much sense, does it?" Howie replied. "I wondered if it wasn't a plant of some kind, but how would that work?"

"I don't know," Bud replied. "I'm beginning to think he was delirious, and it didn't have anything to do with his death."

Bud now pulled to a stop at the large rocks that marked the end of the road. They got out and slowly walked to the edge of the cliffs.

Bud had never really liked this spot, as it was too heady, and he'd always wondered why there was even a road out here—it just simply ended at the cliffs. The road that took off from the River Road a mile or so further south accessed a gravel pit, so it at least had a raison d'etre. That was the road that Graham and Clara and Angus had camped on, and Bud wondered if they'd ever gone back for their tent.

He shrugged. Maybe this little two-track deadend road had something to do with the old missile base. It would be a good spot to sit and watch missiles flying over, and the launch complex was just to the north.

They poked around some, and Bud noted that the winds had erased all the tracks that he'd tried to figure out the last time he'd been there. They found nothing new, and finally both sat on a rock, gazing at the river below.

"Sheriff," Howie said. "I had something strange happen to me last night on my way home."

"What was that?" Bud asked.

"Well, I saw this guy driving along in his car, just some tourist or something, and he saw me and slowed down and put on a space helmet, then waved."

"Did you wave back?" Bud laughed. "That reminds me, I have something for you."

Bud pulled out the photo of the spaceman pointing an egg-beater at him. He'd printed it out and signed it, "To Howie, Yer Cosmic Pal, Bud."

Howie moaned. "Bud, I'm the sheriff. I need to know more about what's going on."

"It's pretty simple, but I'll tell you later—we need to get going," Bud said, standing. "We have just enough time to get out to the rim above June's Bottom before sunset. Don't want to miss it."

But as he stood, he could see a thin white V coming down the river far below, and he knew it was the wake of a boat.

"Looks like someone else is heading for June's Bottom," Bud said, pointing at the jetboat. "I wonder who that might be." He immediately thought of Ryder.

"It could be that Mackie clan," Howie advised. "Or anybody, for that matter. There sure have been a lot of people in town from all this. I had to send a nice family up to Price, as the motels are all full. They couldn't even find a place to stay."

"That's a first for Green River," Bud replied, inching out closer to the edge, trying to see the boat better. "But I doubt if very many have figured out the solstice clue, so I'd be surprised to see anyone there except the Mackie clan and Ryder. He told me that Duncan had helped Angus write that poem, so Duncan should know exactly where it is."

"Why wait until now?" Howie asked, also inching out to get a better look. "If Duncan knows where the treasure is, why not just go get it?"

"Good question," Bud replied. "I've wondered that myself. At one point, he told me that he was looking for a different treasure. I first met him over by the airport, and he seemed very interested in the geyser over there."

"There's a geyser there? I didn't know that," Howie said.

"It's across from the gate, where the tammies are."

"What other treasure would there be?"

"I don't know, Howie. I've given it a lot of thought, and I'm wondering if the treasure in the poem isn't a red herring, and the real treasure is what Duncan's looking for. He had a little map that shows all the geysers."

"But why go to all that trouble to set up a red herring?" Howie asked. They both now stood on the edge of the cliff, watching the jetboat far below.

"I think it has something to do with Ryder," Bud answered. "He told me he's been looking for the treasure for 10 years. He also said that Angus enjoyed the chase—it was a game between the two of them. Unfortunately, I think it's a dangerous game. Someone already got killed, and there may be more..."

With that, the rock Bud was standing on began to slowly tip forward into the abyss, and Bud now knew that he'd finally figured out Angus Mackie's witch's tongue.

36

"It was a good thing I was standing next to you, Bud," Howie said. "And not on the same rock. If I hadn't grabbed you, well..." He gazed into the depths below.

Bud was shaken. It had indeed been a close call, maybe the closest he'd ever come to losing his life, and he owed Howie a big debt of gratitude.

Just as the rock had started tipping and Bud could feel himself tipping forward with it, Howie had the presence of mind to grab his arm and pull him off. They had both almost stumbled forward, but instead had managed to get back away from the rim.

Bud sat on a nearby rock, dizzy and disoriented. His fear of heights, especially in places with nothing to hold onto, was now confirmed as being rational. He was amazed at how careless he'd been, but who would've guessed the big flat rock would tip forward like that?

"So, that's a witch's tongue," he said somberly.

"It's on a fulcrum, Bud," Howie replied. "A smaller rock. As long as you're on the back end of it, you're OK. But the minute you step forward, the balance changes and it tips forward, like a teeter-totter.

The rock's too long and heavy to actually fall off the edge itself, but whoever's on it can sure go flying."

"And that would explain why Angus was lying face down," Bud replied. "The rock started to tip, and he instinctively turned around, and it started tipping back again, throwing him into the rocks. He seemed pretty frail and lightweight, so that would explain how he could go flying and hit his head hard enough to kill him."

"Witch's tongue must be some kind of technical jargon geologists use," Howie said. "I've never heard of it."

Bud now recalled what Ryder had said in the cafe.

"It didn't even register at the time, but Ryder mentioned it when he was talking about the rim on the other side of June's Bottom," Bud replied. "I have the feeling it's an old prospector's term. But I think we now know how Angus Mackie came to be injured, Howie. He wasn't killed by anyone, unless rocks are sentient."

"Rocks are what?"

"Never mind," Bud said, standing and brushing himself off. "We need to get going. We're going to miss the light show. But do you mind driving?"

Howie replied, "That kind of shook me up, Sheriff. I'm never gonna stand out on an edge like that again."

"If you hadn't been, I wouldn't be here right now," Bud replied. "Thanks, Howie."

Bud pulled himself into the passenger seat of the FJ, handing Howie the keys, still feeling off-balance and woozy.

"We're still a ways out," Bud told Howie. "We're going to have to hoof it to get there before the sun sets. Don't worry about bouncing this thing around, it has good shocks and can handle it."

Howie soon had the FJ flying down the River Road, and they passed the turnoff to Fossil Point, then drove by Horse Bench Reservoir, which Bud noted had already almost dried up from the big rain. Before long, they'd taken the turnoff to June's Bottom.

Now the road began to track across washes and occasional tongues of slickrock, forcing Howie to slow down. Bud watched the sun, which was nearing the horizon. He held his hand up, spreading his fingers out between the sun and the horizon, and said, "We have about a half-hour. I hope we make it."

Finally, they were there, and Bud grabbed his camera and binoculars, and they hurried out to the edge of the canyon where they could see down into June's Bottom, which was already in partial shadow.

Holding his binoculars to his eyes, Bud said, "Look down there, Howie. That's where the boat was going, for sure."

A jetboat had stopped on the opposite side of the river below a huge alcove that came down from the rim above, and it looked to Bud as if someone was waiting at its helm, though he couldn't make much out.

"It must be a rented jetboat and boatman," Howie said, also studying the scene through his binoculars.

Now Bud scanned the drainage, and he knew it was the setting for Mackie's poem. He was barely able to make out two people slowly climbing, tracing their way around each concentric ledge, then climbing to the next.

"That looks like a heck of a climb, Sheriff," Howie remarked. "It's interesting how it's been eroded into big ledges by runoff."

"Do you see the guy coming down from the top?" Bud asked. "I bet that's Ryder. It looks pretty sketchy."

Bud now turned around, looking at the sun.

"Howie, get ready. It's time."

Howie turned around and Bud said, "No, keep your eye on the canyon opposite us, where the people are. That's where you'll see it."

Howie asked, "What am I going to see?"

Now the sun began dropping behind the San Rafael Swell on the far western horizon, and Howie gasped. "Bud, look at that! It's a perfect gingerbread man with arms and legs outstretched. How did that happen?"

Bud was now taking photos, wishing he had his new camera and lens. He replied, "It's a shadow man, like in Mackie's poem. It appears only when the sun's at a perfect angle with those rocks over there on the rim, which is only on the solstice. Look to your left and you'll see the rocks."

Bud pointed to a group of high rocks that jutted out from a cliff band above the canyon.

"But Howie, tell me that part of the poem again, the part about the shadow man."

Howie said:

> *It's not a place where one walks free,*
> *But if you search at setting sun,*
> *You'll see the man high in the scree,*
> *His left arm points where search is done.*

"So," Howie continued. "I'm looking where the shadow's pointing with its left arm—Bud, this is too wild. Mackie had to be standing here at solstice just like we are and decided that would be a good place to hide his treasure. And whoever is down there is heading right where the shadow's pointing, so they also know what's going on."

"They don't have much time," Bud replied. "The shadow only lasts a little while, then it fades and you wouldn't know where to look. But I now have photos of it, and I could blow them up and see exactly where to go."

"They're climbing pretty fast, Bud," Howie said, binoculars still at his eyes. "But that guy coming in from the top is going to beat them to it. If they don't get it, we could use your photo and come back tomorrow, right?"

Bud now watched as the person above quickly came around a ledge and dropped down to where the shadow man pointed, just as the light started to fade.

"He's got it!" Howie exclaimed.

"Looks like it," Bud said. He could barely make out the man picking something up and starting back up the rocks. From the way he was moving, it looked like it was heavy, as he had to lift it above him and place it on each ledge, then climb up behind it.

"What about the feet of clay?" Howie asked. "Do you suppose

something bad's going to happen? Remember that part? And the flowing hazards?"

If you are wise and find the way,
Across the hazards as they flow,
Beware of slippery feet of clay,
Walk soft and take in sunset glow.

Bud replied, "It's possible that there's a layer of clay you have to cross, though I wouldn't think it would be too hazardous. But it's steep enough that if you mis-stepped or slid a little, you could start an avalanche. Like the poem says, you'd want to 'walk soft.'"

They stood and watched as the man slowly made his way upwards. But soon, as if in slow motion, rocks and scree began sliding down the steep alcove, tumbling and rapidly gaining in speed and magnitude until the avalanche took him with it.

The two people below now ran to the side to avoid the rockfall.

Bud and Howie stood in silence until the rocks finally stopped in a dust cloud, the man now a good 50 feet below where he'd started, having tumbled off several small ledges. He didn't move, and Bud figured it was from fear of starting the avalanche again or because he was injured, or maybe both.

As Bud and Howie watched, the two people below, who had managed to avoid the slide, now tried to reach the man, and Bud could tell from the way they were gingerly testing the rock that they were worried about it moving again.

Howie said grimly, "Well, it looks like there may have been clay up there and the guy triggered everything into a rock avalanche. Do you think I should call the SAR guys down at Radium?"

"Let's wait a minute and see what happens," Bud advised. "If the others can reach him and get him to the jetboat, it will be a lot faster."

"What happened to the metal box he was carrying?" Howie asked.

Bud replied, "Look at the base of that one big ledge, the one with the juniper jutting from it. See all the gold everywhere? It looks like the box came down with the rocks and broke open."

They watched as one of the people now appeared to be filling their pockets with the gold, which was strewn partway down the alcove. Suddenly, one last sunray reached through a crack in the rim and lit the treasure up like gold lightning, reminding Bud of the black lightning bolt on what would hopefully become Wilma Jean's yellow Piper Cub.

Now the sun had set, and it was almost impossible to make out what was happening. Bud and Howie finally saw a light coming up from the boat, and they figured the boatman had gone up to meet them and help them bring what had to be Ryder down. Before long, they saw the boat's lights come on as it began slowly heading upriver.

"There's nothing we can do now," Bud said. "Might as well go back."

"Let's go meet them at the boat ramp and see if everything's OK," Howie replied.

They got back into the FJ and headed back to Green River as the Belt of Venus, that rose band above the horizon, faded and the stars came out, hanging like rare faceted diamonds in the black sky above as Bud again wished he had his new camera.

37

Howie turned the FJ at the entrance of the Green River State Park, waving as the campground host opened his door to see if he needed to check someone in.

The state park was right across the road from Howie and Maureen's big farm house, and the town's little eight-hole municipal golf course with its huge trees wound between the river and campground, creating an oasis in the desert. It was also the site of the main boat launch for the Labyrinth/Stillwater stretch of the Green River, and it was there that Howie parked the FJ.

"Are you feeling OK, Bud?" Howie asked.

"I'm fine now, Howie. Thanks for driving. It'll take me awhile to process how close I came to dying, and I'm just happy to be here."

"Me, too," Howie replied. "I wonder where the jetboat is."

Just as he spoke, an ambulance backed up to the boat launch. Howie went over and talked to the EMS crew for awhile, then came back to the FJ where Bud waited.

"They got a call from the boatman to come meet them. He said he had an injured party and called it in as soon as the canyon walls got low enough to get cell service. I know it's got to be the people we saw out there, Bud."

"And I would stake my life on those people being Ryder and the Mackie clan," Bud said, pointing to a white Ford LTD parked nearby.

It wasn't long until they could hear the low roar of the jetboat coming up the river, and as it slowly got louder and louder, they could see a light shining on the water, coming towards them.

Soon the boat bumped up to the ramp, and Howie and Bud grabbed the rope as the boatman jumped out and secured it. The EMS team carefully helped Ryder from the boat, who was followed by Duncan and Graham.

It appeared that Ryder possibly had a broken arm, and he was soon inside the ambulance and on his way to the hospital, Graham following in the Ford LTD.

"Where will they take him?" Duncan asked the boatman. "To the hospital in Price?"

"I'm going to guess down to Radium, since it's a little closer," the boatman replied. "It's not as big of a hospital, but for a broken arm, it will be fine."

Duncan, now standing by Bud, shook his head and replied wryly, "He's lucky he's still alive. And for what? For this."

He took a handful of what looked to be gold from his pocket, and Bud knew it was some of the treasure that had fallen out of the box. He handed it to Bud and Howie.

"It's pennies!" Howie said. "Regular old pennies."

Duncan said, "I tried to tell Graham it was fool's gold, just like my grandfather had said in the poem. I helped him write that poem, and I also put the box out there. I knew what I was talking about. But as usual, Graham ignored me."

"Why did you go out there with him?" Bud asked.

"He's so accident prone, I wanted to make sure he would be safe. Clara's the only smart one in the bunch, as she refused to go and stayed at the motel."

"And you knew Ryder would be out there, too, didn't you?" Bud asked.

Duncan looked surprised. "You know Ryder? Yes, I knew he would be there."

"Is Ryder dangerous?" Bud asked.

"Only to himself," Duncan said. "But he's dangerously irritating. He's the reason I had to leave the plane at Sand Wash and float down. He was following me, and I wanted to get rid of him. Gramps put the pennies out there for Ryder as a lesson about greed, but who knows if it worked. He had no idea that Graham would get involved in all this."

"How could Ryder follow you when you were in a plane?" Bud asked.

"I couldn't figure that one out myself. He seemed to always show up wherever I went. I suspect now that Gramps was telling him—I was close to Gramps and called him every day. That's why I hid under your FJ when they were all driving around in Graham's LTD. They were looking for me, and I didn't want Gramps telling Ryder I was out at the airport, as I was planning on going to get my plane. Anyway, Gramps thought the treasure hunt was good for Ryder, said it kept him out of trouble, and it actually might have—well, until now, anyway."

"Ryder told me your grandfather owes him money for a deal they had down in Australia," Bud said.

Duncan replied, "Ha. Some deal. They went down there over 20 years ago to prospect, and my grandfather paid for everything. He invested most of his fortune down there and had the paperwork to show for it. He did nothing illegal or dishonest, and he's been more than fair to Ryder. He actually has a pension set up for Ryder, if Ryder lives long enough to collect it. Grandfather didn't have to do that, and he was always giving Ryder money. He thought the world of Ryder, though Ryder could be a rascal."

"Does Ryder know your grandfather's dead?"

"I told him on the way back. I should've waited until he was recovering, as he took it very hard. As soon as he's out of the hospital, Graham and Clara are having a memorial service for Gramps, then they're taking Ryder back to St. George with them. But Mr. Shumway, do you think you could take me out to the airport? I'm camping in my plane."

Bud sighed. "Duncan, it's really late and we're all tired. Let's just go back to my house, and you can sleep in the Airstream. It was comfortable, wasn't it? I have some longjohns you can borrow."

Duncan replied, "It was fine. Actually, it was really nice. Are you sure you don't mind?"

"I don't mind at all," Bud said. "I won't even know you're out there."

They said goodnight to Howie, who stopped to talk to the campground host for awhile and then walked across the street to his farm house.

Soon back to the bungalow, Bud handed Duncan a pair of longjohns and asked, "Are you going back to St. George, now that all this is over?"

"No," Duncan replied. "Nothing's over. I still need to find my grandfather's treasure. I can't go anywhere until I do, because I don't have any money. Goodnight, Mr. Shumway, and thanks again."

With that, Duncan slipped out the back door and out to the Airstream trailer, leaving Bud to wonder again what was going on.

38

"It might help if I knew what it is exactly that you're looking for," Bud told Duncan over a breakfast of omelets and toast. The dogs sat under the table, begging, until Bud finally got up and gave them each a biscuit, then put them in the back yard.

As Bud sat back down, Duncan replied, "I'd rather not tell you, and you wouldn't believe me, anyway."

"It's that outlandish?"

"In a way, yes. It's very unique. But let's look at the map again. I'm glad you took it off the FJ frame before you went down into June's Bottom, as it would have fallen off," Duncan replied.

"I'm not really that smart," Bud said. "I simply forgot."

Duncan put the map on the table, and they both studied it in silence. Finally, Bud said, "It's kind of like a spider web with Tumbleweed as the center."

"Yes, and I thought that Tumbleweed was of some special significance at first when I saw your note telling me it was a geyser, but now I don't think it is. Gramps loved puzzles, and it was simply a good starting point. But I'd already figured out the letters stood for geysers. I'd been to most of them at least twice, except Tumbleweed and the one by the airport, which I only figured out when I met you out there."

"What does the little poem at the bottom mean?" Bud asked, reading: *Follow the lines, give each a day, and a stubborn Scot can fly away.*

Duncan replied, "I'm not sure, but I think it means I should spend at least one day searching at each geyser to be thorough. The lines would lead me from geyser to geyser. When I met you that day out at the airport and found out there was a geyser there, I thought I'd figured it out—if I'm stubborn enough to find it, and I'm of course a Scot, being my grandfather's descendent, then I would be done and I could leave, fly away in my plane. But that hasn't been the case."

Bud was beginning to have a suspicious feeling, but it just didn't make sense. Could the rose quartz in his pocket be what Duncan was looking for? If so, it didn't seem like much of a treasure.

"Can I ask you a question?" Bud asked.

"Sure," Duncan replied.

"How did you know your grandfather was dead? Graham said you told him and Clara."

"I knew he was dead because I knew exactly where Gramps was at any given time, and his movement had stopped. He had sundowners, you know, and when he finally ended up in the nursing home, he kept getting out, and even got lost once. So I got a GPS tracker, and I put it on his wrist with a bracelet that locked so he couldn't take it off. Both myself and the nursing home could then track him."

Bud refilled their coffee cups as Duncan continued. "When I came down the river, I lost track, but when I got here, I called the nursing home, and they said Graham had taken Gramps on a trip for a few days to visit the country he loved. He spent a lot of time here, you know. That's why he knew about the solstice shadow man. I went down to the library and got online and tracked him to a place out in the desert—that's where they camped—then he was nearby, then didn't move at all, and after some time I could tell he was on the road to Price. He finally ended up at a mortuary and I called them. As next of kin, they and the coroner gave me the information. Do you know who found him? I assumed it was you when I saw the note with his message for me."

"I did," Bud replied. "The sheriff was with me. Angus had wandered off and fallen and hit his head. Graham and Clara looked for him, but couldn't find him."

Duncan said, "They later told me they'd walked everywhere for hours, back and forth on the rim, yelling 'Ang-us, Ang-us' over and over."

Bud looked surprised. "Well that explains that. Someone on the river heard them and thought they were yelling 'help-us.' That's what alerted us to go out there—I work with the sheriff some, as I used to be sheriff here myself. But it was a puzzle, as we thought Angus was the one yelling, and he couldn't have yelled that loud, given his condition. We thought it was maybe a setup of some kind, but now it makes sense."

Bud got up, letting the dogs back in, as they'd started scratching at the door. He asked, "Why did your grandfather hide whatever you're looking for in the first place? I can understand the shadow-man treasure, as he was trying to throw Angus off, but why hide his real treasure? Why not just keep it in a box in the bank?"

Duncan sighed. "It's a long story. Gramps never trusted banks one whit. His parents were Depression era, and he was a Scot, and even though it's a stereotype, there's some truth to the saying that Scots are frugal and independent. After he became wealthy, he bought a nice house and all that for Grams, but most of his fortune was tied up in this Australian thing, not in investments. He said he'd bought it for Grams, but after she died he got paranoid and hid it."

Bud knew Duncan was trying to purposely be obtuse so as to not give away the nature of the treasure, but it did make it difficult to discuss.

Duncan said, "Gramps knew it would continue to go up in value, regardless. He had a little pond out at his place, and he hid it there for a long time. I read later that the British hid the Koh-i-Noor in a pond in England from the Nazis, so maybe that's where he got the idea."

"What's the Koh-i-Noor?" Bud asked.

Duncan replied, "It's the most famous jewel in the world. It's in the Crown Jewels and has an incredible history. But anyway, Gramps decided his 'investment' would be safer out in the desert, so he hid it out here. That was 10 years ago, and when he realized he was getting old and befuddled, he wanted me to have it. He drafted up a will giving it to me, but he told me I'd have to go find it. That's when he gave me the map. I'm not even sure he knew if it was still out there or not. I'm sure he didn't expect to die and was hoping to enjoy the chase second hand, knowing I would call him all the time."

"But he told you what it was, right?"

"Sure. He knew I couldn't find it without knowing what I was looking for," Duncan replied.

"And Ryder knew about it?" Bud asked.

"Yes, Ryder was with him when he bought it down in Australia. It doesn't belong to Ryder. I have the papers showing he purchased it directly from the mine."

"The mine?"

"Yes, for seven million dollars."

"Wow. This was 10 years ago?" Bud asked.

"He actually bought it more like 20 years ago, but he hid it out here 10 years ago. It's worth much more at this point in time. I talked to a dealer a few months ago who told me the largest one known is one-third its size and recently sold for $30 million. When I told him about it, he thought it might be worth $60 million or more, it's so rare. Please don't share that with anyone, though."

Bud reached up and touched his pocket, making sure the rock was still there, then said, "I can see now why you're not giving up the chase."

Duncan continued, "See, Gramps spent several years out in this country prospecting for uranium, and I think that's how he knew where all the geysers were. He'd probably personally found each one. There's no known association with the geysers and uranium, so you know he just stumbled upon them, or maybe he just got interested in them and wondered how they worked, that would be Gramps' style.

He actually did find uranium, but it was down in White Canyon south of here. He later sold his stake, which gave him the money he needed to spend time developing a tire pressure gauge."

Duncan sighed, then continued. "I told you it was a long story. When Gramps gave me the map, he told me two things. He said it was in Green River country, and he also said to never make a copy or let anyone else get their hands on that map. I was to keep it on my own person at all times. I know now he was referring to Ryder. I pretty much memorized the map, but when I realized that Ryder was following me, I knew I had to put it someplace safe. I'd seen you out working in the field, and I knew I could find you again, so I put it on your FJ. I had no idea you were an ex-lawman. Like I said, I had the map memorized, but just one misstep would sink the whole thing, so I wanted to be able to refer back to it if I needed to, otherwise I would've destroyed it."

"Why didn't he just give you the treasure?" Bud asked.

"I was too young," Duncan replied. "My mom had passed away—he was very fond of her—and this was to be my inheritance, and Graham and Clara would get the house and some stocks and things like that. But I was just a kid when he hid it."

"Why go to all the trouble to put a bunch of pennies in a metal box, write a poem about it, then give it to *Treasure Magazine*?" Bud asked.

Duncan laughed. "Well, when Gramps got the wild hare for all that, he was still an active guy, not yet in the nursing home. One reason he and Ryder were friends is they're both kind of rascals like that, and he decided to play a little joke on Ryder, who was always saying he'd been swindled and the treasure was his, even though he knew better. It was a game he and Gramps played. So, I helped him write the poem, then went down the river in a jetboat and hid the box, which was no small task, believe me. Gramps drew a picture of exactly where to hide it—he did that from memory of seeing the shadow man, which I find impressive, as he was an old guy at that point. Then Gramps called *Treasure Magazine*."

Duncan now shook his head. "Of course, everyone knew he was

wealthy, so they ate it hook, line, and sinker. He knew it would irritate the hell out of Ryder, and he also knew that Ryder would get all involved looking for it. I don't think he had any idea how many others would also take up the search. It was all a ruse, a way to make Ryder think the diamond was in the box."

"The diamond?" Bud asked.

Duncan stammered as Bud reached into his pocket and pulled out the supposed rose quartz.

"Is this what you've been looking for?" he asked.

For a moment, Bud thought Duncan might pass out, but instead, he simply closed his eyes as if he couldn't believe what he was seeing.

39

Bud sat in the back booth of the Melon Rind Cafe, drinking coffee and reading the *New York Times*. Since Green River didn't have a newspaper, Wilma Jean had a subscription and always left it laying around the cafe for people to read. Bud figured it was so everyone would realize how good they had it in the little desert town.

The cafe was back to normal, and Bud figured all the treasure hunters had given up, now that the solstice was over.

He was surprised to see Art and Nick walk in and take a nearby booth. They nodded hello, and Bud said, "I take it you're going back out with the BOB-O's."

The pair wore faded denim shirts with colorful designs on the collars and cuffs, as well as worn jeans with iron-on knee patches, and wide leather belts. Art had a large belt buckle with a giant beehive on it with the word, "Utah," and Nick wore what looked to be a well-worn pith helmet.

"We got a new vehicle—an old Scout—and we're set to meet up with everyone in an hour at the museum parking lot," Nick replied.

"Where are you going?"

"Everyone decided June's Bottom was too difficult to get to, so we're going on over to Temple Mountain and camp on the Behind the Reef Road," Art said. "Come along with us, Bud."

"Thanks, boys," Bud replied. "But my orange plaid pants are in the wash. Besides, I need to get caught up down on the farm. But you're going to have a great time. That's fantastic country over there. I just hope your sleeping pads aren't too terribly old."

Wilma Jean said hello to Art and Nick, then sat down across from Bud, removing her sandals and putting her feet up on the booth seat alongside him, wiggling her toes.

"Hon," she informed him, "My feet hurt. I'm not going to sell the cafe after all. Me and Vern came up with a better solution than my buying his plane with money I don't have."

Bud had been reading about how some bank in Chicago had been fined millions of dollars for something or other, and it made him think of Angus Mackie and how he didn't trust banks. His mind then drifted to Mackie's memorial service out at Lover's Leap.

He replied, "Boy, that was some service they had, wasn't it?"

Wilma Jean said, "Oh, you mean for Mr. Mackie? Yes, it was. His nephew playing the bagpipes out there on the edge of that canyon was really something. I've never heard *Amazing Grace* played so well, and he looked so nice in the Mackie tartan. And then when you and Howie blasted that rock off the edge in Mackie's honor—what did you call it, a widow maker?—well, that was something too. Did you notice how the echoes just went on and on, all the way down the canyon?"

"It was a witch's tongue. But what did you think of the photos I took with my new camera gear?" Bud asked.

"I could see a significant improvement, hon," she replied. "But did you hear a word of what I just said?"

"Sure," Bud said, turning back to the paper. "You said it was a nice service, and you liked the piping, and..."

"And I'm trading half of the bowling alley for Vern's Piper Cub. Did you hear that part?" she asked, irritated.

Bud set his coffee cup down, looking at her. "You're doing what?"

"We made a deal," she replied. "I need someone to take over—I'm too tired to keep doing it all, plus I want to fly more. Vern's wife is bored stiff and wants to be around her grandkids. They're moving up here, and she's going to run the bowling alley and they'll own half and I'll help some and we'll split the profits accordingly. Vern's going to see if he can get a flight school going here—and a fuel pump. Isn't that great?"

"And you're not selling the cafe? I worried about it for nothing?"

"I could easily find something else for you to worry about, if you'd like," she smiled.

"I can keep my back booth and come in and eat apple pie?" Bud asked.

"The booth, yes, the pie, maybe not so much."

Bud grinned. "This is great news. But did you see this article today about the Desert Rose?"

"Isn't that the diamond you stole from the Mackies?" she teased.

"It is," Bud said. "Did I tell you Duncan said he was going to send me a reward? It's going to easily cover my camera gear. Isn't that nice of him?"

"How can he afford that? I thought he had to sell the diamond before he had any money."

"Well, according to the paper here, it just sold. He'll have plenty of money now. Listen to this."

Rare Diamond Brings Rare Price

What's possibly more valuable than the exquisite Koh-i-Noor, the 105-carat diamond set in the Crown Jewels of Great Britain and the source of bickering between Great Britain and India for years?

Well, there's a new contender in the ring—the Desert Rose—a fabulous 15-carat extremely rare red diamond from the Argyle diamond mine in Kimberley, Western Australia. According to Sotheby's Auctions, the Desert Rose just set a world record for the highest price per carat at a stunning US$5 million, for a total price of US$75 million.

Why so expensive? The Desert Rose, which was recently offered from the estate of Angus Mackie of Utah and was mined over 20 years ago, is the rarest color of diamond ever found. Until the Desert Rose came on the *scene, the largest red was the 5.11-carat Moussaieff Red Diamond. These so-called fancy diamonds, such as the deep-blue Hope Diamond, are among the most valuable and sought-after jewels in the world. Before the Desert Rose, the Pink Star, a 59.6-carat pink diamond, was the most expensive fancy diamond ever sold at auction at US$71.2 million.*

Red diamonds are the most expensive and rarest diamond color in the world and will typically run in the hundreds of thousands of dollars per carat range. It is difficult to find them in large sizes, and most are less than one carat. Owing to their high price range, red diamonds are generally purchased by diamond investors or collectors. Of all diamonds, red diamonds are the only ones whose size of under one carat will not disqualify them from being an investment stone, since so few red diamonds larger than that can be found on the market.

And who was the purchaser of this remarkable diamond? Sotheby's isn't telling, but rumor says it's the British royal family.

"That's somewhat unbelievable," Wilma Jean said. "How can anything be worth that?"

"It's all perception," Bud answered. "Value is in the mind of the perceiver. And if you perceive and have enough money..."

"A fool and his money are soon departed," Wilma Jean said, getting up. "Just like Angus Mackie—gone—so what's the point? But someone should remind the Queen about all those jewels she already has all locked up. And hon, I can't believe you carried that thing around in your pocket. It didn't even look like that big of a deal, but fiddling with a $75-million diamond kind of takes the cake, doesn't it? But I need to get back to work. Are you going to get the dogs and go back out to the farm?"

Bud nodded yes as she stood and went into the kitchen, but he was in reality far away, thinking about the Desert Rose and the close relationship they'd had not all that long ago.

He knew it had been a once in a lifetime experience, the apex of his fiddling life, and he knew he could never top it, no matter what might come along.

If there were a magazine devoted to the art of fiddling, he knew he himself would be worthy of a full edition, maybe called, "The Fiddling Hero," and he'd be the one that other fiddlers would emulate and never surpass, and his would be a record that would stand the tests of time forever, like a rare 15-carat red-diamond tiara.

It was something he would never forget, he mused, leaving a tip for Maureen. And yet, it all seemed kind of unreal.

All in all, it hadn't really been all that different from having a big faceted piece of rose quartz in his pocket, and his old rabbit's foot had done just as good of a job as a fiddling device when it all came down to it, until the dogs had chewed it up.

But they would never be able to chew up something like the Desert Rose, so maybe in that respect it was worth something, Bud decided, putting on his hat.

He walked out the door and on to better things.

ABOUT THE AUTHOR

Chinle Miller writes from southeastern Utah and western Colorado, where she spends most of her time wandering with her dogs. She has a B.A. in Anthropology and an M.A. in Linguistics and an A.S. in Geology.

If you enjoyed this book, you'll also enjoy the first book in the Bud Shumway mystery series, *The Ghost Rock Cafe*, as well as the second, *The Slickrock Cafe*, the third, *The Paradox Cafe*, the fourth, *The No Delay Cafe*, the fifth, *The Silver Spur Cafe*, the sixth, *The Ice House Cafe*, the seventh, *The Rattlesnake Cafe*, and the eighth, *The Beartooth Cafe*. This is the ninth book in the series. The next will be *The Cessna Cafe*, coming soon.

And don't miss *Desert Rats: Adventures in the American Outback, Uranium Daughter*, and *The Impossibility of Loneliness*, also by Chinle Miller. If you enjoy geology, try Chinle's *In Mesozoic Lands: A Guide to the Mesozoic Geology of Arches and Canyonlands National Parks*.

And if you enjoy Bigfoot stories, you'll love *Rusty Wilson's Bigfoot Campfire Stories* and his many other Bigfoot books, as well as his popular *Chasing After Bigfoot: My Search for North America's Most Elusive Creature*.

Other offerings from Yellow Cat Publishing include an RV series by RV expert Sunny Skye, which includes *Living the Simple RV Life, The Truth about the RV Life,* and *RVing with Pets,* as well as *Tales of a Campground Host*. And don't forget to check out the books by Sunny's friend, Bob Davidson: *On the Road with Joe* and *Any Road, USA*.

Made in the USA
San Bernardino, CA
30 October 2018